SALVATION

CASSIE LAELYN

Title: Salvation

Author: Cassie Laelyn

Cover: Bookcoverology

This book was originally published in 2020 as part of the Warlords, Witches and Wolves anthology.

Two destinies. One curse. A secret to die for…

Return to Woodland Falls, pack up the past, and get the hell out of there. After fifteen years, it should be easy, right? Sure, until Mia Jones stumbles into the town's sexy bartender, Noah Cole. His wolfish grin and impossibly bright blue eyes trigger a forgotten memory, throwing her plans into a spin. But when she discovers Noah's secret, their reunion goes from destined to deadly.

Now, she must choose between her heart and preventing an ancient curse that threatens the entire shifter community.

But what if those she loves are the biggest threat?

For those who believe in second chances.

ALSO BY CASSIE LAELYN

The Fallen Guardians

Unforsaken (Book 1)

Unforgotten (Book 2)

Unseen (Book 3)

Untamed (Book 4) coming 2021!

Small Town Packs

Salvation

Reclaim

Awaken (coming soon!)

prologue

Mia
Age Fourteen

Day One in Woodland Falls.

I tossed my jacket on the bed. The one with a paisley pink bedspread to match an equally pale pink room that made me want to hurl. A room fit for a girly-girl, who surprise, surprise, wasn't me.

A summer's worth of belongings sat in an unopened suitcase at the foot of said vomit bed. I stared at it for longer than I should, but I couldn't bring myself to unpack. Unpacking meant accepting that my mother dumped me here.

Why? A question I asked myself a million times during the drive. Every time, the answer was the same. Mom had better things to do for the summer. Even now, she and the grandmother I only just met, argued about something downstairs. Probably her ditching me or how I was such a disappointment to her.

Apparently, my grandmother's name was Joan. Also apparently, it slipped my mom's mind to introduce us earlier. Like, anytime during the last fourteen years.

Life sucked. Correction, *my* life sucked.

A door slammed downstairs, startling me. Shortly after, a car engine started then drove away.

I guess Mom left.

I just stood there. Empty. So many thoughts collided together that the hurricane of emotion opened a gaping hole inside my heart.

Outside the room, the floorboards creaked as someone ascended the stairs. Part of me hoped the foot-steps belonged to Mom, even though I knew better. This wasn't the first time she'd dumped me.

When Joan appeared in the doorway, my throat went all scratchy, but I refused to cry. I wouldn't give Mom any satisfaction, even if she weren't here to see it. Instead, I jutted out my chin.

I always asked Mom if I looked like my dad, who I'd also never met because my mother forgot to introduce us as well. Mom and I had the same dark brown hair, but the resemblance ended there. Now I knew why. All my looks came from Joan. We had the same hazel eyes, same round face, same fat bottom lip, though I didn't have a set of wrinkles at the corner of my eyes like her. I guess I would someday. If Joan's hair wasn't salt and pepper and cut in a short bob, I bet it'd look the same as mine.

"It'll be okay, Mia," Joan said from the doorway.

I wasn't convinced. What kind of mother left their kid with someone they only just met? Instead of saying that, I opted for silence.

"Why don't you get settled? I'll go make us some supper."

Without waiting for a reply, Joan returned downstairs. She seemed nice. But then, when I was younger, so did my mother.

For the next ten weeks, I'd officially live in the middle of nowhere. A town so tiny the population didn't even match the number of people living in a single suburb in Seattle.

With a dramatic sigh, I trudged to the suitcase. If I left it closed, I'd never change my clothes. Forever living in sweats and a T-shirt I could handle, but never sketching again? That was a big fat no.

I clicked the combination and unzipped the case, grabbing my sketch pad.

Movement outside the window caught my eye. Abandoning the sketch pad, I moved to the bay window to peer outside. Late afternoon shadows drifted over the brown-green lawn. Procrastination was by far my best superpower. Luckily, I didn't need to focus too much for good grades. Maybe I got that from Joan as well? If so, I was glad for it because summer school would suck worse than being here. Marginally.

Out the window, a tire swing hung from a branch on the nearest pine tree. I imagined sitting there all day sketching. Even Joan's freshly baked chocolate-chip cookies wouldn't entice me to socialize. I knew she'd make them. Didn't all grandmothers?

Nothing seemed any different from when I peered out the window half an hour ago. As I turned away, a flicker between two trees stopped me. I leaned closer to the glass, squinting.

Wispy fog rolled between the branches, spilling onto the lawn. Did this place even get summer?

I scanned the yard, past the dead, overgrown vegetable patch, to the shed. As soon as I walked in the house, Joan told me her one and only rule: stay out of the garden shed. Weird, but whatever. I wasn't into gardening anyway. Clearly, she wasn't concerned about me exploring the forest though, given her unfenced property extended right to the tree line.

I followed the tree line back to the spot right outside my window. My breath caught. A large animal stalked between the trees, heading toward the house.

From my spot looking out the second story window, it resembled a dog only much bigger. As though it sensed me watching, its head jerked in my direction. My heart leaped into my throat and I jumped back.

Great. Wild dogs lived in the forest behind Joan's house. Now I couldn't even use the tire swing.

Once my heart stopped pounding, I inched closer to the window and took another peek. With its gaze locked in my direction, the animal stepped closer to the yard. Slowly, more of its body became visible. A long, narrow nose. I gravitated closer to the glass, kneeling on the window seat to get a better look. Dark, almost black fur. It must be a wolf. I'd never seen one in the wild and I never expected they were so...breathtaking.

The wolf stalked closer, now only a few feet from the grass. Wolves were predators, hunters, but Joan's yard only offered dead plants. What did it want?

I considered calling out to Joan, but a strange sensation stirring in my middle made me remain silent. The wolf inched further forward, hesitant to step on the grass but evidently compelled to do just that.

My hand itched to sketch the magnificent creature, my fingers twitching to rake through its glossy fur. A fierce black wolf here in Woodland Falls.

It didn't act like a predator. Maybe this place wasn't so bad after all.

"Mia?" Joan beckoned from downstairs.

Mesmerized by the wolf and a yearning to see its whole body, a reply stalled in my throat. I couldn't take my eyes off it, let alone turn away.

I held my breath as the wolf breached the tree line. With my palm flattened on the window, I leaned forward until my breath fogged the glass. I sent a silent plea for the wolf to come closer. To rescue me. Then I wouldn't spend an entire summer vacation alone in a dreary, country town.

When the wolf lowered its front paws on the grass, it stilled. Waited. Like one of those cowboy standoffs. The wolf met me halfway and my turn was next. A weird thrill I only ever got during art class made me ache to run downstairs, burst out the back door, and into the forest. I could forget why my mother dumped me here. I could run away and live in the woods.

Just me and the wolf forever.

"Mia?"

I squealed and spun to find Joan standing in the doorway. That woman was stealthy.

She smiled. "Didn't you hear me calling you?"

Yes. "Sorry, I was looking at..."

"At what?" She frowned and stepped inside my room.

That stirring in my gut intensified, telling me to keep my new friend a secret for now. At least until I knew Joan wouldn't call someone to take the wolf away or worse, shoot it with the shotgun hanging on the wall by the back door. If that happened, I'd never see it again and my forest escape plan would fail before it even began.

"Nothing. It was nothing."

She waited a few seconds before nodding. "All right. Supper's ready. Come down before it gets cold."

"Sure."

As her footsteps trailed back down the stairs, I peered out the window to where the wolf halted a few seconds ago. Only now, it was gone.

chapter one

Mia
Fifteen years later

I pulled into the gravel parking lot of Cole's Bar and Grill. I hadn't been back to Woodland Falls in what felt like forever. After that one summer, my poor excuse for a mother left me home alone. I guess I should've thanked her for at least coming back for me. Though, countless times, I wished she had left me with Joan. The second I could move away to college, I did, thanking all the gods above for my art scholarship. Without it, I wouldn't have an education. Or a life.

I killed the engine. Heavy rain pelted the car with no

end in sight. I considered waiting in the car until it slowed but the sooner I met with the lawyer dude, the quicker this trip ended. I eyed the entrance to the bar. If I ran, I might make it inside semi-dry.

I grabbed my purse from the passenger seat and draped my jacket over my head before opening the car door and bolting to the entrance.

This town had two seasons: freezing cold or stormy.

I halted just inside, shook the rain from my jacket and brushed my fingers through my hair. Once I thought I looked semi-respectable, I surveyed the bar. The lawyer said he'd wear a navy sweater, which narrowed it down to about six patrons. I tucked my purse under my arm and scanned the faces, not that I knew what the guy looked like. I'd only spoken to him twice on the phone.

On the far left, I spotted a long bar with empty stools. Rather than waiting by the door, I'd sit there, and the lawyer could find me. After a full day road trip, I was in serious need of a drink.

I weaved between a few tables with the bar in sight until a guy called out from my right.

"Miss Jones?"

Clearly, an out-of-towner was easier to spot than a lawyer wearing a navy sweater. I swung around and found a guy waving from a booth along the outer edge.

Navy sweater: check.

I diverted to his table. "Ashton?"

"Sure am," he said, holding his hand out. "It's nice to officially meet you."

"Likewise." I shook his hand. "Sorry I'm late. The drive was longer than I expected."

"Don't worry about it. This isn't the worst place to wait."

He gestured for me to sit, and I slid into the booth, stowing my soaked jacket and purse in the empty space beside me. "The rain's pretty wild out there."

"Welcome to Montana summers." He chuckled. "This shouldn't take long, then I'll give you the keys and you can get dry."

"That'd be great."

I glanced toward the bar, unsure why. Liquor bottles lined the wooden shelves resembling any other bar. But a weird feeling tugged at me. A sense I'd been here before, which I knew wasn't the case. I doubt the bar was here when I stayed with Joan that one summer.

Shrugging it off as fatigue, annoyance, frustration, and every emotion I could think of, I turned back to the lawyer. "What do I need to sign?"

From an old-fashioned leather briefcase, Ashton pulled out a large envelope and handed it to me.

"There are two copies. One for you to sign and return to me, the other is yours."

My heart thudded. People died all the time, but it never happened to someone I knew. Though, it shouldn't surprise me. Tragic was obviously my family's middle name.

I stared at the envelope in my hands.

"Did you know her well?"

I shook my head. "I hardly knew her at all."

I wasn't the most gracious teenager. Could anyone blame me? From the age of ten, I practically raised myself. Why did that poor old woman have to die? Why couldn't Mom...

I halted that thought. Sure, my mother continually treated me like an outcast, but I wouldn't let my shitty childhood define me any longer. I was an adult who made my own choices. Including the choice to disown my sorry excuse for a parent the second I walked out the door for college.

With a deep breath, I slid the paperwork from the envelope and lay it face-up on the table.

"She left you her entire estate. The property, house and its contents."

I peered at the document with my name on the front page. I didn't want the house or anything inside it. I just wanted to sell everything so I could set myself up properly. Pay off my billion dollars of debt. Okay, a slight exaggeration, but the way those bills hung over my head made it feel like billions.

For me, this was my fresh start. A chance to stand on my own two feet and stop living paycheck to paycheck.

"Where do I sign?" I rummaged through my purse for a pen.

"I tabbed the pages. Take it with you and drop it back to me tomorrow once you're happy with everything."

No time like the present. Before Ashton went all lawyer on me, I flipped to the final page and signed and dated where indicated.

The poor guy almost fainted. "Wait! You haven't read the conditions."

I shrugged. "Would it make you feel better if I agreed to read them tonight?"

"No, because you already signed it."

"I'm not going to contest anything. As soon as I put the place up for sale, I'll be out of here."

I gave him what I hoped was a reassuring smile.

His cell rang, and I'd never been so grateful for the interruption.

He shifted to grab the cell from his pocket, then held it to his ear. "Ashton Cole."

I pivoted in my seat to give Ashton some privacy while he spoke on the phone. Country rock music played in the background, loud enough to hear, but soft enough to still have a decent conversation. The place wasn't half bad. Kind of a mix between a bourbon bar in the city but with a small-town vibe. Two patrons sat at the bar, with the rest scattered at the round tables and a handful of booths.

That strange sensation through my middle drew my gaze back to the bar. More accurately, the guy behind it. Dressed in a black T-shirt and jeans, his tall, lean body reached for a bottle of liquor from the highest shelf in a move that stole my breath. With his back to me, I couldn't see his face, but I didn't need to. I was too busy checking out all his ink. Dark tattoos covered one arm all the way to his wrist, the ink flexing and coming to life with each movement. The guy had a naturally built body. No bulging veins or crazy, pumped biceps that barely fit beneath his shirt. He had toned muscles strengthened by years of manual labor rather than hours in the gym like most of the guys I knew these days.

Naturally toned physiques had sadly become a thing of the past in the city. This guy was a refreshing change.

As though he sensed me mentally stroking his arms, the guy stilled. His shoulders rose with a deep inhale. His head tilted slightly, and I shifted in my seat, anticipating him turning my way. I bet he was downright gorgeous.

"I'm so sorry," Ashton said, startling me. He slid out of the booth with his briefcase. "I have to head out."

I forgot he was even there. "That's fine." I gathered my things and joined him to stand.

He shook my hand again. "Promise me you'll read over the paperwork and call me if you have any questions."

"I will."

He turned to leave. "Oh, I almost forgot." From the briefcase, he fished out a set of keys and handed them to me. "These are yours."

The second my fingers closed around the keys, Ashton released his grip and left. I stood there for a few more minutes staring at them in my palm. The last time I visited that house I left behind my only regret.

chapter two

Noah

"Who's the newcomer?" Liam nodded to the brunette chatting with Ash.

I shrugged, acting as though I hadn't noticed, but I couldn't deny it. My heart stalled the moment she strolled through the door.

I marked the bottle of bourbon off the inventory sheet and placed it back on the top shelf.

"And why is she meeting Ash?"

"Dunno." I reached for next spirit on the list.

Liam slid a carton of beer on the bench and slapped

my shoulder. "Don't tell me you haven't noticed. I caught you watching her."

"Don't you have somewhere to be?"

The little shit smirked. "Nope. Ivy's in Timber Falls with Kat."

I inwardly groaned.

Liam opened the carton and stocked the beer fridge. "You should jump in there before someone else beats you to it."

Here we go...

"It wouldn't kill you to get out there. You know, date a little."

"I date."

He stared at me with a deadpan expression. "Dating the bar doesn't count."

Sure, it did.

"All you do is live here and pine over a girl you've never even met."

I grabbed a nearby tumbler and poured a shot of bourbon. One advantage to owning the joint. "I'm not pining."

Just because I gave my heart to someone fifteen years ago and never moved on, didn't equate to pining.

Liam narrowed his ice-blue eyes. All three of us had the same eyes. My mother called them "the Cole eyes," thanks to Dad having a matching set. Not hard to tell we were all related.

"You saw that girl fifteen years ago. What if you never see her again? Will your relationship with the bar be enough for the rest of your life?"

I turned back to the shelf. Those same questions

plagued me ever since I first spotted her. That summer she ventured into the forest every afternoon until, one day, she didn't. If only I'd had the balls to shift into human form and let her see me in person rather than hiding behind my wolf.

Maybe then, I wouldn't have become so complacent.

Ready for this shitty conversation with Liam to end, I spun and faced my younger brother. "How long did you wait for Ivy?"

Liam sighed. "That's different and you know it. Ivy and I have known each other since I was twelve. You know, in person, not from afar."

"It doesn't matter anyway. She'd never forgive me." I shot back another mouthful of bourbon to ease the pressure building in my chest. It didn't help. Nothing ever did.

Liam's strong hand squeezed my shoulder. "You gotta stop blaming yourself. It wasn't your fault."

Not from where I stood.

I swallowed the lump in my throat and remained silent. After an awkward as fuck moment, Liam released his hold.

"That's the last of the beer. You want me to close?"

Without turning, I shook my head. "Nah. See you tomorrow."

To avoid constantly staring at the newcomer, I kept busy with inventory, marking items off like a robot. Why did my whole family have an issue with me dating my bar? I had my chance with a mate, and I screwed it up before it even began. Shifters only got one. No point in searching for another.

"Excuse me?"

I spun and nearly landed flat on my ass. The woman who met with Ash hopped up on a barstool. My wolf uncurled and stretched as though waking from a decade-long hibernation. For a split second, light flared through my chest. *Was she...?* Then reality kicked in and snuffed it out. The universe already gave me my chance and I missed it.

I pushed the emotions aside, flung the dishtowel over my shoulder and got my shit together.

She was pretty. Delicate features, a beautiful smile, deep hazel eyes that were all mysterious in the low light. Her dark brown hair tumbled over the tightly wrapped scarf around her neck. Even though that girl stole my heart fifteen years ago, I could still appreciate a beautiful woman when I saw one.

She placed her purse on the bar top and scanned the shelves behind me. "Okay, bartender, hit me with your best cocktail. No cream."

This, I could do. The dating shit? Not so much.

For all his flaws, and the list was fucking long, in this case Liam was right. I was more than happy to date my bar until they buried my ass on the Cole ranch. Dating a bar came with only two complications: taxes and suppliers who couldn't keep their word.

Dating women who weren't *her* felt like living a lie.

I flattened both palms on the bench. "You're not in the big city anymore, darlin'. Folks here think people who drink cocktails also add soda to their bourbon. And..." I screwed up my face to emphasize my point. "What crazy person adds soda to bourbon?"

That made her smile, lighting up her eyes. Weird sensations sped through my veins and my wolf purred like a damn house cat. Now wasn't the time for it to pounce around. Besides, this woman wouldn't stay long. No one from the city ever did.

"I wouldn't want to get on the wrong side of the locals by having such an outlandish drink choice."

I held back my smirk. "Wise move."

"Okay, in that case, I'll have bourbon please. Straight up."

I grabbed my favorite and poured her a nip, placing the glass on a napkin in front of her.

She reached for her purse, but I held up my hand. "It's on the house."

"Are you sure?"

I nodded. "Think of it as a reward for choosing wisely."

"Whew. I'm so relieved."

I almost snorted.

"I'm Mia." She tipped her glass in greeting.

"Noah." I grabbed a tray of tumblers from the washer and began drying them. "So, Mia, what brings you to Woodland Falls?"

She tapped the envelope beneath her purse. "I'm just here for a few days to tie up loose ends." She sipped the bourbon. "It shouldn't take long."

"Not keen on staying?"

Why the hell I asked that, I'd never know. The quicker she left, the better. I had a feeling this woman could coax not just my wolf from hibernation, but me too.

If that happened, she'd want something my heart couldn't give.

"It's not that, it's just...I don't know. It's strange being here."

I stacked a few glasses and kept drying. "How so?"

"I haven't been here for years." Her lips rolled inward into a flat line. "It doesn't matter."

I wanted to ask why, but it wasn't my business. She mustn't have stayed long the last time she came to town. Woodland Falls was so small someone couldn't sneeze without everyone finding out about it. Plus, I'd lived in this town my entire life, if she ever lived here, I'd remember.

She was probably a city hotshot looking to make a few bucks. Times were tough in small towns across Montana, but never tough enough to sell to some city slicker.

Even though I knew I should leave her to it, I wanted her to keep talking. Her voice soothed something in my soul. Just because I didn't date didn't mean I wasn't lonely. No, lonely wasn't the right word. I was happy on my own. At times though, I wished for a conversation with someone who didn't know my past.

Or my mistakes.

Mia cleared her throat, moving the tumbler aside to grab the envelope. "I guess I should read this. Ashton almost had a fit when I signed the papers straight away."

I chuckled. "That sounds like him. He likes rules."

"I gathered that. But the sooner I get this over with, the sooner I can get back to Seattle."

Knew it. A city slicker wanting to make a quick buck.

Mia slid paperwork from the envelope and started reading. That was my cue. Most people who sat at the bar wanted to chat for whatever reason. They yearned to offload their guilt over a bourbon, sought reassurance or needed advice. I loved owning Cole's bar for those exact reasons. The sense of companionship, comradery. The ability for someone to divulge their secrets, so they didn't eat them alive.

Pity, I couldn't do the same.

To give her some privacy, I wandered to the main seating area and gathered empty plates and glasses. The kitchen staff did a stellar job keeping the main area serviced, but every now and then I enjoyed the break and it gave me a chance to chat with the locals.

"Are you freaking kidding me?" Mia squawked.

I stilled, torn between finding out what happened, and giving her privacy. In the end, the need to make sure she was okay won.

I rounded the bar. "What's up?"

She waved the documents in the air. "This. This is what's up."

I frowned, waiting for the punch line.

"Ugh!" She shoved the documents back in the envelope and gathered her purse and jacket in a flurry. "Do you know where Ashton's office is? I need to speak to him right now."

I grabbed my cell from my ass pocket and checked the time. "He has an office on the main street, but he won't be there at this time of night. I can call him if you like."

"No, it's fine. I'll call him." She threw her hands in

the air. "I can't believe I was this stupid." She slid off the stool. "Thanks for the drink."

Urgency to make her stay slammed into me from nowhere. I couldn't let her leave. And it had nothing to do with her being the first woman in fifteen years to capture my attention.

Okay, maybe it did.

"Wait." I tossed the dishtowel on the counter. "It's pouring outside. Let me drive you."

"To Ashton?"

"Yeah, he's my brother. He lives out of town and the roads are unforgiving in weather like this."

She scanned the bar. "Don't you need to be here?"

I waved off her concern. "Nah, someone else can close for me."

Her shoulders dropped with a heavy exhale. "That'd be great. I don't exactly know my way around."

"Just give me a second." I grabbed my cell and dialed Liam. He answered on the first ring.

"Yeah?"

"Something's come up. I need you to close for me."

Given Liam's silence, clearly his brain tried to figure out the reason behind my request. I barely held back a giant eyeroll anticipating how much shit he'd give me.

"Hmm. Does this have anything to do with a certain brunette in the bar tonight?"

"Will you close or not?"

The shithead chuckled. "Yeah, on my way."

chapter three

Mia

Rain still pelted down in wild sheets. I tucked the envelope inside my jacket and raced behind Noah to his truck. Once seated, I clutched the envelope in my hands so tight it crinkled the edge.

How could I be so stupid? Ashton told me to read it first. I just didn't think there'd be conditions to my inheriting Joan's estate. _Who does that?_ I thought this chance was too good to be true, that my sucky luck finally changed. Nope.

Noah's truck grumbled to life, and he drove out of the

parking lot. The wipers swished like crazy, clearing the windshield.

"Are you okay?" he asked once we were out on the main road.

Yes. No. Not really. In less than an hour, I'd arrived in Woodland Falls, signed a will without reading it, and now I sat in a truck with a stranger. Stupid on all counts. Yet, a feeling in my gut told me Noah wasn't a stranger. Like in the movies when two people knew each other from another lifetime. I didn't know. But I sensed no danger. And usually I was a pretty decent judge of character.

Though, could I trust my gut right now? I just signed a freaking will without reading it.

"I'm sure it's just a misunderstanding." *I hope.* "I appreciate you driving me."

His gaze swung to me and then back to the road. "No problem. Ash lives on the outskirts of town. It's hard enough to find during the day, let alone at night with this rain."

I nodded. Small talk was never my specialty, even more so now.

The poor guy took pity on me and didn't push for a conversation. Instead, he turned on the music and kept his eyes on the road. Every now and then, I sensed him glance over at me. I clutched that envelope and prayed for a way out of this.

Noah turned off the road and continued down a long drive before stopping in front of a beautiful old farmhouse. Lights lit up the wrap-around porch. Three stories, shutters on the windows, wide timber steps. Even with the horrid weather, the place was straight out of a home magazine. On a sunny day, I bet the house was stunning.

"Clearly being a lawyer pays well," I blurted. Sometimes, I really should keep my mouth shut.

Noah snorted. "It's actually an old family home. But you're right, lawyers charge like savage wolves."

As Noah killed the engine, the front door opened and Ashton stepped onto the porch, dressed more casually than when I saw him an hour ago.

I tucked the envelope under my jacket again and ran for the house, straight up the steps onto the porch.

Ashton held open the front door. "Come inside where it's dry."

I flipped off my muddy shoes and darted inside. By now, there was no hope for my jacket, so I left it outside. Just before the door closed behind me, I swung to Noah holding back on the porch. "Are you coming in?"

"I'm good out here." He settled into one of the chairs like he owned the place. "Take your time."

He drove me here and didn't seem fazed waiting outside on the porch while I dealt with this disaster. I'd never met a guy with such old-fashioned manners and chivalry. Another refreshing change.

Once I closed the door, Ashton offered me a towel, and I dried my face and hands.

I followed Ashton through the grand foyer to an office off to one side. Instead of taking a seat behind the large mahogany desk, Ashton sat in an armchair and gestured to the other. "I take it you read the condition."

I sat on the edge of the seat and slipped the will from the envelope. "Can she really do this?"

"She can and she did."

A heavy weight sank in my belly. "Surely, there's a way out of it?"

"I'm afraid not." He thought for a moment. "From what I know, Joan hoped you'd build a life here in Woodland Falls. This is your opportunity to try it out before you consider selling her estate."

Build a life here? My mother tainted all my memories of this town when she dumped me here for an entire summer. No matter how hard Joan tried to make it enjoyable, that underlying resentment lingered in everything I did. Regardless of what condition she included in her will, I'd never move here.

The only thing that kept me together the summer I came here was the wolf. The mysterious creature that reappeared in the forest behind Joan's house every afternoon. That wolf became not just my friend, but my salvation. It wouldn't surprise me if I created the memory as a coping mechanism for dealing with my shitty childhood.

I exhaled a long, tired breath. "What happens if I don't adhere to the condition?"

I asked the question even though I suspected the answer. The hard line on Ashton's mouth confirmed it.

"The estate will be sold, and all monies donated to the local animal rescue, as stipulated."

I hung my head for a moment to compose myself.

I couldn't stay here. What would I do for work? I doubt my boss would give me the summer off. He'd probably use it as an excuse to fire me. I had savings, but they were for emergencies. Was this an emergency? Staying at Joan's house was rent free, so I wouldn't need to pay that on top of the apartment I shared with an old college friend back in the city.

Maybe it could work. Sure, it wasn't in my plan, but when had anything in my life gone to plan?

Okay. I could do this. Another eight weeks. After that, I'd sell the house, pay off my debt and finally set myself up.

"All right." I stood and slid the will back inside the envelope. "Thanks for seeing me again, especially at your home."

He stood, giving me a warm smile. One that brightened his eyes. I didn't notice before, but Noah's eyes were the same shade. An intriguing ice blue with flecks of steel gray.

Ashton led me to the porch where I found Noah sprawled in the chair like he and the furniture were well acquainted. Noah's eyes drifted open and my heart skipped a beat. He was a goddamn vision relaxed in that chair.

He peeled himself up to stand. "All sorted?"

"As much as it can be." After I slipped on my ruined shoes and grabbed my jacket, I turned to Ashton. "I guess I'll see you round town."

"Sure will."

Noah tipped his chin at Ashton before we darted to his truck. Once back inside, he started the engine and drove out the way we came.

A few minutes down the road, I couldn't hold back the tears. They poured out of me like the downpour of summer rain. Wild and never-ending. I rummaged through my purse and grabbed a tissue. One. That wouldn't last long but I used it anyway, mainly for my nose which decided to join the party.

Before I could stop him, Noah pulled the truck off the road and put it in park. He pivoted to face me but didn't say anything, just waited for my embarrassing outburst to do its thing.

When the tears slowed and no longer threatened to drown us, I wiped my nose with the soggy tissue and gave Noah the best smile I could muster.

Deep grooves creased his brow. "Did Ash upset you?"

I shook my head, my mind working overtime. *Nope.* My mother did this. If she never introduced me to my grandmother, I wouldn't have wanted more in life. I never would've inherited her estate. I wouldn't be back here.

Rain pelted the truck, the sound ten times louder while stationary. I stared out the passenger window into the darkness, wondering what my life would've been like if things were different. If Mom didn't neglect her only child, ditching me at every opportunity. If Joan fought to keep me after I stayed that one summer. Or if I'd called her from time to time rather than resenting her for letting my mother take me back.

The downward spiral threatened to pull me under. This time, I almost let it. Would it be so bad?

Yes. Years ago, I refused to let the past define me. I refused to become my mother. Mia Jones was better than that.

"Sorry." I let out a weak chuckle, not sure why.

Maybe to lighten the mood? I wiped the wetness from my cheeks and glanced at Noah. "I bet that's the last thing you expected when you offered me a ride."

I gave him a smile, hoping to alleviate some awkwardness.

He didn't seem convinced. Ever so slowly, he wiped a tear away with the pad of his thumb. The touch so faint and tender, it made my heart ache anew.

"Don't ever apologize for feeling."

His hand stilled on my cheek and I closed my eyes for a moment, sinking into his touch.

"What can I do?"

"There's nothing you can do." No one could fix this. I just needed to get through this roadblock and then start fresh.

The remainder of the summer. Eight weeks.

"Do you want to talk about it?"

Did I? Not usually, but with Noah, maybe I did just a little. But talking about it and letting him in, created complications I wasn't ready for and attachments that wouldn't last.

Attachments never lasted.

He lowered his arm. Instead of pulling back, he took my hand in his, giving it a light squeeze. "You don't need to. I get it. It's much easier solving problems over bourbon."

This guy could read me like a book and we'd only just met.

I peered at the envelope I'd tossed on the truck floor. "Things haven't exactly gone to plan, that's all. I'll be fine."

His eyes narrowed, studying me. The intensity of his stare burned through layers of flesh and bone right to the heart of my soul. I swallowed, composing myself. "Really. I'm sorry about that. I don't know what came over me."

"Stop apologizing."

As the rush of my tears and emotions slipped back into their perfectly crafted box, another sensation bloomed inside my chest. Heat from Noah's hand cradling mine spread through my veins, awakening my senses. I inhaled his wild, earthy cologne and calmness washed over me all the way from my muddy shoes to my fingertips and back again.

In the dim light of the truck, his eyes drew me in until I forgot why I cried in the first place. I could easily lose myself in those eyes and that scared me more than anything else.

"Do you have somewhere to stay?"

"Ah...yeah."

Noah cleared his throat and slipped his hand from mine, snapping me from the trance.

"How about I drop you off and you can pick up your car tomorrow? It'll be safe at the bar."

"That'd be great."

Noah started the engine and pulled out onto the road. "Where to?"

"I'm staying at my grandmother's house. Um..." I grabbed the envelope at my feet and checked the will. "There's no address. It just says the Whitcome property on Cobalt Lane."

The truck jerked toward the curb, then righted again. "You're Joan Whitcome's granddaughter?"

"Yeah. Did you know my grandmother?"

Noah's grip tightened on the steering wheel, so slight that if I hadn't already been looking at him, I would've missed it.

"Something like that," he muttered.

chapter four

After dropping Mia at the Whitcome property, I slid the truck to a halt in front of Ash's place. My place. *Our* place. *Whatever.* Ever since the...incident, I'd slept upstairs at the bar. I'd rather that than face my brother's disappointment every fucking day.

I got out and slammed the door as a warning to Ash in case he didn't hear the truck roar down the drive. As I marched to the steps in the pouring rain, the front door opened. My older brother stepped out, followed by Liam. Both of them.

Just fucking great.

"Why the fuck didn't you tell me?" I roared at them. Though, Liam probably just found out. He was guilty by association.

Ash stepped forward. "I told you I found who Joan left her estate to."

"You said a woman from the city. You never said it was her granddaughter," I yelled, remaining under the deluge so I didn't punch Ash in the face. Every inch of my clothing clung to my skin, but I didn't give a shit.

"No fucking way," Liam muttered.

Ash raked a hand through his perfectly styled hair. He peered at the rafters, inhaling a deep breath while I mentally counted to ten.

"I didn't know, I swear. The will had her name, no relationship. Given she has a different surname and isn't married, I assumed they weren't related. You know how long it took me to find her."

I threw my hands in the air. "It's her. Don't you get it? She's the girl. It's Joan's fucking granddaughter."

I sensed a connection to Mia the moment she strolled into the bar but didn't want to acknowledge it. Or hope. It explained why my wolf stirred, and when she cried, a sudden need to protect her nearly floored me.

I glared at Ash, trying to control the urge to knock him on his ass. I never used my fists to take out my frustration, but right now I reassessed that life choice.

"What the hell did you say to make her cry?" I growled.

Ash crossed his arms over his chest, his lawyer expression fixed into place. "You know I can't tell you that. Besides, I didn't intentionally make her cry."

"Argh!" I shouted, turning to the forest.

The same forest that connected Joan's place to ours. The same forest our wolves ran through. The same fucking forest where that sick psycho hunted.

Mia was on the other side of those woods in Joan's house for the first time in fifteen years and I couldn't even stomach going there.

Liam and Ash remained silent as I tore a track in the muddy grass. The rain slowed to a drizzle, dripping down my face. For so long, I prayed the girl would return or the universe would give me a clue how to find her. We had one summer of fleeting moments where each afternoon, I shifted and crept into the forest to wait for her. Even now, my damn wolf purred at the memory of Mia running her fingers through his coat.

Then one day she never showed. But I still held onto hope. Now, all that hoping blew up in my face.

Mia was a Whitcome.

I spun to face my brothers. Liam sat on the porch swing, while Ash leaned against the closed front door.

I trudged up the stairs out of the rain and lowered my voice. "Don't you think it's screwed up that the universe fated me with a Whitcome?"

With the heel of his sneaker, Liam rocked the swing back and forth. "Let's hope she's like Joan."

"What if she isn't?" I looked to Ash. He always had the answers. "What the hell do I do then?"

"If she's your mate, things will work out as they're meant to. If not...we should prepare ourselves."

I glared at the idiot. "She is my mate. Don't ever doubt that."

Ash was the responsible one, but also the most cynical.

This situation was beyond screwed up.

I collapsed in the same cane chair I sat in earlier. "This is karma for not protecting Joan."

Ash pushed off the door and sat in the chair beside me. "Joan's death wasn't your fault. We've discussed this. Besides, the universe fated you with a Whitcome long before she died."

"What if she figures out how her grandmother really died?"

"She won't," Liam answered.

I leaned my head against the backrest and stared at the rafters for a long moment. This mess not only involved my brothers, but also the bar, Woodland Falls and the whole shifter community. "This is a fucking nightmare."

I practically heard the cogs turning in Ash's mind.

"Our safety wasn't guaranteed forever. We knew that. And you probably have a few months tops before she senses what you are. If you want a future with her, you need to put what happened with Joan behind you and figure out how to make it work."

I side-eyed Ash. "And how do you suppose I do that?"

"She's here for at least the remainder of the summer, that much I can say. Use the opportunity to make peace with this. It's time you stopped punishing yourself."

My mouth fell open. "Are you suggesting I go about my business as though nothing happened?"

"That's exactly what I'm suggesting."

"She's my mate. How do you expect me to lie to her?"

Ash didn't miss a beat. "Not telling and lying aren't the same thing. Her grandmother died unexpectedly. If you don't say anything contrary to that, everything will be fine. She told me she hardly knew Joan. She probably doesn't even know what she is which could work in our favor."

Trust the lawyer to say something like that.

My stomach twisted into thick, tight knots. Mia was here to mourn the death of her grandmother. I couldn't face her for the entire summer hiding those secrets. Did she know about the shifter world? About her family?

Would she even remember the wolf she befriended as a kid? Were the memories burned in her brain like they were in mine?

How could I face her without telling her what I did?

Liam stretched his legs along the swing. "Why don't you use the summer as your penance? Make amends for what happened. That way you're not lying, you're earning her forgiveness. You're setting things right."

Setting things right.

Those three words rolled around in my head. That might work. I wish Liam would stop acting so mature. He was my younger brother, not the other way around.

If Mia was here for the summer, I could use that time to get to know her, and she could get to know me. That way, when the timing was right, I could find out if she knew about the shifter world.

Hopefully then, she wouldn't kill me.

chapter five

Mia

Summer started last week. What great timing my grandmother had. I guess it didn't matter when Joan died, the will stated I needed to spend a summer here before I sold the estate. One whole summer.

Who confirmed I adhered to the will's conditions? Ashton? I should probably find out.

After my little episode last night in Noah's truck, and a good night's sleep, I now thought a little clearer. I wandered downstairs, taking everything in with fresh eyes. The house was nothing like I remembered from the summer I spent here. Though, as a resentful teen, the house had only resembled another prison.

Faded, chipped paint, hairline cracks in the ceiling, dated window furnishings. The farmhouse needed repairs here and there but from what I could tell, nothing major. Joan died almost two months ago and given the thin layer of dust, no one tended to the inside of the house in her absence. Someone maintained the gardens, which saved me some work.

Ideally, I'd hire someone to complete the repair work before putting the house on the market. But money wasn't exactly bursting from my pockets. At a minimum, if I wanted a reasonable price with a quick sale, the house needed a thorough cleaning and declutter. That only cost my time, which I now had plenty of.

First, I needed to collect my car from the bar and apologize to Noah for last night. The poor guy all but threw me out of his truck when he dropped me home. I mean, I would too if a stranger burst into tears in my car for no apparent reason. At least the rain stopped sometime during the night, which made for a dry walk to the bar. After that, I'd start cleaning.

Everything felt better with a plan.

I grabbed my coat but pulled up short when I opened the front door.

Noah strode up the stairs with a takeout cup in each hand. When his gaze lifted to mine, my breath stalled. His eyes were impossibly bright during the day. Such a contrast to his raven hair and groomed short beard.

"Hey."

That strange feeling I got when I first arrived at the

bar returned. A sense we'd known each other before, even though we'd only just met. Maybe we were kindred spirits because I'd remember him if we'd ever met before now.

In an unrelated thought, why was I so comfortable with him turning up at my house?

Weird? *Maybe.* Cute? *Definitely.*

I closed the front door behind me. "Hey, yourself."

Last night, I noticed his good looks, but now, in the light of day? He was hot. Like insanely hot. Rugged male with small-town charm.

He wore a T-shirt and jeans combo as though the cool weather didn't faze him. Locals probably thought this was a heatwave. Once again, my gaze zoomed in on all that ink. The forest on his forearm seemed so lifelike, with a river flowing through the middle, and a single black wolf near his wrist.

Maybe I sensed our connection because he also liked wolves.

"Coffee?" He handed me a cup.

A light chuckle bubbled in my chest. "I take it coffee is an acceptable beverage choice?"

"Second only to bourbon."

His lips kicked up at the corner, revealing a deep dimple. Just when he couldn't get any hotter, he went and did that.

"Good to know."

I sipped the coffee and moaned as the caffeine registered on my tongue. Joan's house was devoid of edible food. Before I climbed into bed last night, I threw out everything in her fridge, so I didn't accidentally poison myself sneaking a midnight snack.

Noah hitched his chin toward his truck. "Want a lift to the bar?"

Switching the coffee between my hands, I slipped on my jacket. I should invest in a rain jacket if I needed to stay here for the summer.

"Thanks. Saves me walking." We jumped into Noah's truck and he started the engine. "This is becoming a habit, you driving me around."

His fist tightened on the steering wheel. "Every little bit helps."

Huh? I pivoted to ask what he meant but stopped. Although he offered to drive me, the frown and pained expression on his face said he wasn't too pleased about it.

Luckily, Joan's place was only a few minutes from the bar and grill.

Noah pulled up beside my car in the parking lot and I fished out my keys.

"Thanks for the lift," I said, hopping out of the truck and closing the door.

He rounded the hood and met me on the passenger side, leaning one arm on the truck all casual and sexy as hell. "The bar doesn't open until midday. I can make you breakfast if you like."

"Oh, ah...you don't have to, it's fine."

The guy was clearly being hospitable, but there was no need. I'd made it in the world alone long enough to manage on my own. Besides, I didn't want to give him the wrong idea. As soon as the summer was over, I'd head back to Seattle.

"I'd like to." He pushed off the truck and started walking to the bar, ending any further protests on my behalf.

"Okay."

But only because caffeine wouldn't keep me going for long.

I followed Noah inside and waited by the door while he switched on the various lights. "Do you open the bar early for all the new girls in town?"

"Only you."

My stupid heart flipped at his words. This wouldn't end well.

"Besides, I own the place, so I can open whenever I want."

Of course, he owned a bar. I should've figured that out by the name. He wasn't just some ordinary guy, from an ordinary family, living an ordinary life. He probably swooned all the newcomers.

"How long are you here for?" he asked, walking behind the bar to switch on the last set of lights.

"The summer." I dumped my purse on the top. "I inherited Joan's estate when she died." I sighed. "That was a bit too much information for first thing in the morning."

Noah stilled, facing the liquor bottles, his head angled to the floor. "No. I'm sorry."

"It's fine. I...hardly knew her."

I kept saying that, and each time it tugged more at my heart.

He turned to face me. "The death of someone important to you is never easy."

I sensed he spoke from experience, but I refrained from asking. Death wasn't exactly the happiest breakfast subject.

After a moment of silence, Noah left the main bar area and walked into what I presumed was a kitchen.

"What's your plan for the Whitcome place?" he asked through the open door.

I stood by the bar, tracing my fingernail along a grove in the timber. "I'm going to sell it once the summer is over." When he didn't respond, I filled the silence. "Joan included a condition in her will that states I need to live in the house for a summer before I sell it. It needs a little work and a big declutter, but I think it should sell. It's a beautiful home." The smell of salty bacon lured me through the door into the kitchen. "Anything I can do?"

He pointed to an egg carton. "Could you pass me those?"

I did, and Noah cracked a few into a bowl and whisked them with a dash of cream.

"A man that can cook and bartend, where have you been all my life?"

He gave me that dimpled smirk over his shoulder. "Waiting."

My heart stilled. Those words, the intensity in his eyes. How could someone I'd only just met have that effect on me?

Focusing back on the hotplate, he poured the egg mixture into the pan. "What repairs does the house need?"

I laughed, mainly to ease the pressure building in my chest. "Don't tell me you're handy at DIY, too?"

He shrugged. "I do all right. My brothers and I took over the family ranch when our parents died."

That pressure returned tenfold. His parents died. I disowned my mother and never knew my father. With all these things we had in common, no wonder it seemed like we'd already met.

"I'm sorry."

"Don't be. They lived a long and happy life."

I leaned against the counter, content with watching Noah. He transferred the mouthwatering fry-up onto plates and lured me back out to the bar.

Seriously, where had this guy been my whole life?

Noah set two places for us, and I sat on the stool beside him. "Thanks for this."

"Anytime." He grabbed a fork and dug in. "You know, Woodland Falls may have shit weather ninety percent of the time, but there's lots of hidden gems only the locals know about." He paused, chewing a piece of bacon. "If you're here for the summer, I'd be happy to show them to you."

Warmth bloomed along my cheeks. This guy made me smile more in the last twelve hours than I had in...forever.

Would it be so bad to spend time with him while I completed my mandatory will-cation? *No.* Quite the opposite. I suspected spending time with Noah would make the summer much more enjoyable. And maybe, just maybe, it'd ease some of my guilt for never contacting Joan when I had the chance.

I glanced at him and smiled. "I'd like that."

chapter six

Noah

Ivy settled on a stool, eyes tracking Liam as he rounded the bar to stand in front of her. "Soda?"

Ivy nodded. "Can you put a piece of lime in it?"

"Anything for my two favorite girls."

I stilled, dishtowel in my hand, gaze darting between Ivy and my brother. "Wait? You know what you're having?"

Ivy rolled her eyes. "No. But your brother is convinced it's a girl."

Liam shrugged. "I know it."

I flipped the towel over my shoulder and zoned out as

the two of them bantered back and forth at the odds of having a girl. As far as I knew, the odds for shifters were the same as humans. Fifty-fifty. Given Ivy was human, until the little one hit adolescence, no one knew if they would shift. I suspected Ivy hoped for a shifter, but I doubted Liam gave a shit. He just wanted to have a family with his mate.

Liam moved to stand beside me as I filled the coffee filter. "Have you found out if she knows yet?"

"I'm working on it."

Over the last week, Mia dropped into the bar every day for a chat or coffee, other times for meals. I loved how our relationship effortlessly bloomed into friendship. Easy, relaxed, no pressure. So far, the plan to earn her forgiveness had worked. But she never spoke of her family and I'd seen no sign she knew about the shifter world. I think a big part of me avoided the topic because I didn't want to know the answer. What if she knew?

But I couldn't avoid it forever. Which was why yesterday, I finally grew the balls to suggest I take her to one of the town's hidden gems.

Liam nodded, but the hard set of his jaw told me all this waiting and not knowing stressed him out. He not only worried for Ivy, but also for his unborn child. We all did.

"You better get going or you'll be late."

I checked the time on my cell. "Shit. You're still good to stay?"

"We're fine." Ivy cooed. "Go and woo your mate."

"She's not officially my mate."

Yet. Hold up. When did I start making forever plans with Mia? *Fifteen years ago, dumbass.*

Ivy waved her hand, dismissing my words. "She will be. Now go."

I turned to Liam. "She has more bite than you."

"I heard that!" Ivy growled.

The corner of Liam's mouth twitched, his eyes darkened, a sign he and his wolf were in sync. Not just about Ivy having more bite than him, but that Ivy was his perfect mate. The other half to his soul, the one person in the universe destined only for him.

I'd given up hope of ever having that. Instead, over the past few months I'd come to terms with being the cool uncle. I stopped allowing myself to wish for something more.

But now, everything had changed. Mia came back into my life causing all that hope to drift to the surface. I just needed to get through these obstacles, pay my penance, figure out what she knew, and then we could have our forever.

I snatched my keys off the counter and walked out from behind the bar. Halfway to the door, my phone rang. I dug it from my pocket and Ash's face flashed on the screen.

I lifted the cell to my ear. "Yeah?"

"Baker just came to see me."

Not a second later, the door to the bar opened and Baker strode in, removing his baseball cap as he walked toward me. The bulky shifter was from the wolf pack in Timber Falls. They made shifters the size of trucks over there—wide, strong and impossible to move.

"He just walked in. What the hell's going on?"

Shifters from other packs visited every now and then, but the tight expression on Baker's face told me this wasn't social.

"Baker will explain. I'm heading to Timber Falls to meet with Rhett. I'll call you after."

Ash ended the call, and I shoved my phone back in my pocket. Shit must be real if Rhett, the Alpha of Timber Falls, sent his second in command to speak to us. My chest tightened. The last time that happened was the night we lost our parents.

Since Dad died, Ash became Alpha of our pack. Not that our pack was huge but being the eldest meant that responsibility fell on his shoulders. Plus, Ash was better at dealing with shifter politics.

Baker acknowledged Ivy with a chin tip, then turned to Liam and me. "You boys got a minute?"

The guy was lucky Ivy didn't punch him in the face for excluding her. Being a human didn't stop us from including her in shifter matters. Though, today she seemed content to stay seated with her fizzy drink.

"Sure, come out back," I said, pocketing my keys.

Ominous clouds swirled in the pit of my gut as I led us past the kitchen to a small office.

Liam followed and closed the door behind him. No one bothered sitting.

"What's up?"

Baker got straight to the point. "He escaped."

My stomach slammed against the floor.

"Fuck." Liam glanced at the door, no doubt concerned for Ivy and their baby's safety.

I clenched and unclenched my fists. "When?"

"Last night."

"How the hell did he escape? I thought your pack had him locked up?"

"I'm investigating it. Listen, I doubt he'll show his ugly face around here for a long time, but don't let the wolves out for a bit just in case. At least until we know it's safe."

Easier said than done. I could control the shift, push my wolf back inside his cage if I needed, but when it came to protecting my family or someone I loved, my wolf didn't always obey.

"Joan's granddaughter claimed her estate." I needed to say it, get it out in the open so we were all on the same page.

Baker's expression softened. Pity was an understatement. I hated that look. I'd seen it for the past fifteen fucking years.

"Ash filled me in. I'm sorry, man."

Great, now that another pack knew, news would trickle across to the neighboring towns until the entire shifter community sent me sympathy cards for the holidays.

"I gotta get back." Baker slipped on his cap. "Let me know if that asshole shows up. Next time, we won't be so forgiving."

Baker gave me a curt nod and Liam a friendly slap on the back before leaving.

I glared at Liam, rage bubbling beneath my skin. "I should've killed that bastard."

By the time I pulled up in front of Joan's place—now Mia's place—Mia sat on the front porch in a pair of jean shorts and a T-shirt, waiting. My chest squeezed with a mixture of excitement, anticipation. Concern and worry. Fucking dread.

I had less than seven weeks left to make this work with Mia. Creating opportunities for her to get to know me and to trust me was the first step. That way, when I told her the truth, she'd believe it and hopefully choose us.

Now that psycho had escaped, and no doubt sought revenge.

I couldn't think about that right now. Mia was my mate, and I needed to focus on that connection for this plan to work. Ivy suggested I woo her, which was easier said than done. This shifter was out of practice in the wooing department. To be honest, I doubt I was ever in it.

As Mia walked to the truck, I pushed my fears aside and focused on the present. I opened the passenger door for her. "Excited?"

She dropped her bag in the truck. "I'm a little nervous. Why the hell do I need a swimsuit?"

"To go swimming."

She hopped in. "It's only seventy degrees."

"That's a heatwave here." I laughed, closing the door, and settled into the driver's side. "We don't get many, so we seize the moment whenever we can."

I backed down Mia's drive and out onto the main road, heading to the other side of town. My heart wouldn't let up. Having her in my truck again, with her sweet night jasmine scent filling the space, made my pulse crazy. My hand itched to reach over and hold hers, the urge so powerful it overtook every other thought. But for now, I held back.

"I feel like you're my personal chauffeur."

"You're new in town. Driving is easier than directing from the passenger seat."

Plus, driving helped her. *Pay my penance, seek forgiveness.* Added to the list: keep her safe.

When I turned onto the Cole driveway, Mia's gaze darted to me. "Hang on. Isn't this Ashton's place?"

"Actually, it's the Cole family ranch."

"You live here, too?"

"Nah, only Ash lives in the house now. I live upstairs at the bar, and my younger brother lives with his mate... ah, *wife*, in their own house on the far side of the property."

She relaxed back in the seat, nodding to herself. "That's why you looked so comfortable on the porch the other night."

Memories of my mother rose in my mind. "I have a thing for porches. There's nothing better than sitting there watching the world go by." I drove past the house then diverted off to the right, following a dirt track. "Growing up, I used to sit out there with my mom every morning. We'd just chat about whatever. It became our thing."

"You're lucky your mom actually cared."

I almost asked about her family, to find out how much she knew, but before I could, she changed the subject.

"So, you know this secret place because it's on your family's land?"

"Yep. You're the first non-Cole to go there."

Besides Ivy, but ever since Liam met her when they were kids, we considered her family.

My grip tightened on the steering wheel as we entered the forest using a well-worn track. My body switched to high alert, searching for threats. Sensing the change in adrenaline, my wolf paced back and forth, waiting to shift. I prayed it wouldn't come to that. I planned to show Mia what I was, but not today.

"Is that because normal townsfolk refuse to swim when it's freezing?"

I snorted. Weather had nothing to do with it. Having all the kids in town playing on Cole land wasn't safe, especially when, at any moment, a wolf might unexpectedly join the party. But I couldn't tell her that, yet.

We drove through the forest until the road ended in a small turnaround where I parked the truck. "We have to walk from here."

The second I got out peace washed through my blood. It happened every time I immersed myself in the forest. Regardless of the possible threat lurking in the woods, this place always soothed my soul. Pine needles, crisp air, earthy scents. Wolves were drawn to nature, probably why packs lived in small towns rather than big, populated concrete cities.

That fucker wouldn't take that away from me. He'd already taken enough.

I led Mia deeper into the forest, following a dirt track. She remained silent for most of the walk, commenting every now and then on a patch of wildflowers, or the height of a towering tree. I relied on my heightened hearing and smell, constantly sifting the air for danger, pretending everything was fine.

When the gushing water grew louder, a burst of energy swirled in my gut. We were almost there.

I needed Mia to feel the connection between us for my plan to work. If I told her straight up who I was, and she didn't know about our world, I risked her leaving for good. Then I'd lose her again. If by chance she already knew, showing her my wolf form could result in fatal consequences.

I wanted her to stay. I wanted this to work. I couldn't wait another fifteen years, especially after seeing her again.

Mia trailed close behind me around the rock formation, pausing as we came to a hidden clearing.

"Surprise." My voice a little gruffer than usual.

"It's so beautiful," she whispered.

Crystal clear water gushed down a mossy rock formation, into a deep pool. Standing beside Mia, I inhaled a full breath filled with fresh, pure water, earth, and her. Her scent wrapped around me like a warm summer night, attaching itself to every inch of my skin. My wolf stirred, torn between curling up like a sleepy kitten and protecting her from possible threats.

This time when my hand reached for hers, I didn't hold back. I slipped my pinkie around hers, shooting a wild thrill through my blood. She took it a step further and curled her whole hand in mine. My breath bottled up deep in my chest, a familiar warmth expanding through my middle. The same feeling I experienced every time I thought of her.

Hope.

Hand in hand, I led her to the bank and dumped our bags near the narrow stream. "It's spectacular after all the rain we've had this week."

We stood there for a moment, admiring the view before I slipped her hand from mine and flipped off my shoes. I grabbed the hem of my shirt and lifted it.

"What are you doing?"

I paused, shirt half off. "Swimming?"

"Oh, right. Obviously." She peered at the waterfall, biting her bottom lip. "It looks cold."

I stripped off my shirt and tossed it by my shoes. "A little fresh maybe."

"Don't lie. That's code for freezing."

My laugh ended abruptly when I sensed Mia's gaze, burning a path over my body. I didn't dare look. Not yet. I couldn't let her know how much she affected me. Having her so close after so long, a second chance, an opportunity to right my wrongs. A chance to finally be happy.

She grounded me like only a mate could, giving me more peace than the forest. I needed that every day for the rest of my life. But I hated not telling her what I was or worse, what I'd done. The more I avoided it, the harder it would be.

I pushed those thoughts aside and walked down to the water. The second my toes hit the freezing abyss, my balls shriveled up and died. Jesus, I hadn't swum here since I was a teenager. Clearly, the entire time I was drunk or just plain stupid.

Regardless, I couldn't back out now. I'd committed to swimming, and I never backed down on a commitment. No matter the cost.

The first few steps were always the hardest. In life and in this damn pool. Teeth clenched, I inched further into the water until it reached my knees.

To hell with it.

I dove in. An invigorating rush burst over my body, stealing air from my lungs. When I resurfaced, I wiped the water from my eyes and spun to face the bank. Mia stood there, her arms hugged across her middle, in a goddamn scrap of fabric.

chapter seven

Mia

"C'mon, it's not that cold." Noah waved me over from the middle of the water.

I held back. "I call bullshit."

He laughed and dove under again, flipping on his back to float. I could stand on the bank and watch that all day long.

My hesitation wasn't just the freezing water. The strange feeling swirling through my body was now front and center, and I could no longer ignore it. This guy was a freaking god, with or without clothes. Not that I saw beneath his shorts, but I didn't need to. His upper torso was enough to turn a girl's legs to jelly. Perfectly formed biceps, hard toned abs, and tanned skin dipped in glorious tattoos. Noah might just be the most gorgeous guy I'd ever laid eyes on.

He stood, rising out of the water and strode toward me looking like he belonged in a secret agent movie. "It's fine once you're in."

I still called bullshit. But my new life was about seizing the moment. Not letting opportunities pass me by. I'd regret not getting into the water. More than that, I didn't want to see his disappointment if I said no.

"Okay." I lowered my arms, stepped to the water's edge, and dipped in a toe. "Holy freaking cow. It's ice."

Noah barked a laugh. Before I knew it, he stood in front of me. How did he move so fast? Despite the water's temperature, heat radiated from his body, all that firm skin covered in tiny water droplets. My eyes tracked a single drop as it slid all the way from his chest to the hem of his shorts. I should stop drooling over his abs. My hand twitched. I wanted to trace the drop's path, tuck my fingers beneath the hem of his shorts and yank them down.

Oh, no way. The last thing I needed was to fall for this guy. Clearly, my body didn't get that memo.

I dragged my gaze back to his. His light blue eyes darkened until they resembled the deepest depths of the pool behind him. Dark and mysterious. It must be the light because I'd never seen eye color change like that.

My breath quickened. As though in slow motion, he lifted his hand and swept it along my jaw. Even though we'd only just met, his touch felt familiar, awakening something deep inside me.

He leaned closer. My heart galloped. He was going to kiss me. I wanted him to, but should I? I'd only known him for nine days. Not that I counted.

He drew closer still until his warm breath whispered along my lips. I closed my eyes, anticipating his mouth touching mine.

In one swift movement, he scooped me off my feet and flipped me over his shoulder fireman style. I squealed, kicking my legs, but that only encouraged him further. He dashed back in the pool, carrying me until the water lapped at my feet.

Pressed against him with all that body heat swirling over me, didn't distract me enough. The water was still cold.

"Ready?" His tone was deeper, raspier than a moment ago.

I swallowed, so I could at least respond. "No?"

Without waiting a second longer, he dropped to his knees and dunked us both beneath the water. Air punched from my lungs in one whoosh. My fingers tingled. Goosebumps burst along my arms and legs. I kicked, trying to get free but Noah tightened his hold.

Less than a second in the water, he stood again. I sucked in a breath.

He slid me down his front, still holding me tight. "See? It's not that cold."

Not now, not against his chest. Of course, I didn't say that aloud. Too lost in his eyes, I didn't care what happened outside our little bubble. My whole body wanted to curl up next to him and bask in his warmth forever.

As though he only just now sensed the intimacy of our position, Noah lowered my legs for me to stand. I retreated a few steps, stumbling over uneven rocks until the water reached my shoulders, but he followed, never more than an arm's length away from me. His gaze locked on mine.

"You're right." I spun to face the waterfall, pretending to admire it instead of thinking about how much I wanted his hands all over me. "It's warmer once you're in."

He moved behind me. Goosebumps transformed into tingles, sweeping through my body, centering in one place.

He pressed flush against my back and lowered his mouth to my ear. "Wanna see behind it?"

I seriously needed to compose myself. "Behind the waterfall?"

"Yeah."

Beneath the water, he took my hand and led me toward the falls, following a path around the outer edge.

"I could carry you."

Carrying me wasn't a good idea given how my body reacted last time. I needed to put space between us before I burst into flames. "How 'bout I race you instead?"

His wicked dimpled grin curled on his mouth a second before he dropped my hand and dove to the waterfall. *Damn cheat!* But the joke was on him. From where I stood, I'd already won. Watching him, the way those muscles in his arms and back flexed with each stroke, made a girl drool. Especially this girl.

I took my time, following the same path as Noah to one side of the falls where I treaded water, admiring the fresh, misty spray hiding Noah behind the falls. He held out his hand, guiding me behind them.

On the other side, he boosted me onto a ledge made by a natural groove in the rocks. The view from behind the waterfall was nothing short of magical. Sun sparkled and glistened in the water. Toasty warmth from the rock spread along my skin, making me want to hide here all day.

Oh, wait. That heat came from Noah.

He settled in beside me, hands curled over the ledge, feet swinging back and forth in the falls. Water sprayed in every direction.

I couldn't wipe the grin from my face. This place was the coolest, I could hide out here forever.

"Okay, the water's cold, but totally worth it for this view."

"Great rewards come from great sacrifice."

He said some strange things. "Pity we didn't bring snacks."

He glanced at me and something expanded in my chest.

"I have some in the bag. You want me to get them?"

I shook my head, torn between feeding my stomach and not wanting this moment to ever end. The more time I spent with Noah, the more I imagined a different life. One where everything was simple, easy. That I had a normal upbringing like him. A life where I stayed with

Joan instead of going back to Seattle with my mother. Maybe then, Noah and I would've met earlier. Maybe then, this would have worked.

I wiggled my toes, splashing water over my legs. Noah's body radiated so much heat that before long, my goosebumps disappeared.

I easily imagined a life here. An alternate life with someone like him.

Without a shirt on, his tattoos were on full display. The forest art continued up his arm, past his elbow to his shoulder. A large wolf's head spread along his shoulder, with a smaller one covering the spot over his heart.

"Tell me the story behind your ink."

A hint of sorrow swept his face before he shrugged one shoulder. "I love wolves."

"You have a lot of them. Are they like your spirit animal?"

He shifted, hands clenching and unclenching on the rock. I guess the tattoos meant something to him. Maybe they were symbolic, representing someone he lost or loved. Maybe he adored wolves like me.

"Wolves are pack animals. They value and protect family above everything else."

Now I got it. Family was important to him. If I had one, I imagined it would be important to me, too. "Just like you?"

"Something like that."

"But this one is alone, like it's lost in the woods." I traced my finger over the smaller black wolf near his wrist. My heart pounded. Him touching me seemed natural, comfortable, as though he'd done it hundreds of times. But when I touched him? That zapped little pulses of heat straight through my middle.

His gaze lowered to my finger then back to me. "That's a lone wolf. One without a mate."

"Without a mate?"

He peered at the waterfall. "Wolves mate for life. Once they find the one for them, they don't let go. But every now and then, a wolf doesn't find their other half." He paused a moment, glancing at his toes dipped in the water. "That tattoo represents the wolf who never found its mate and instead, wanders the earth alone."

Morbid much? "That's kinda sad."

The pain behind his eyes made my heart ache. I sensed there was more to the story, more to the lone wolf, but all thought disappeared when his gaze lowered to my lips. My heart sped to that delicious point right after I finished sketching a picture, where I stood back to admire my handiwork. The moment where my chest swelled beyond belief realizing I'd created something magical and beautiful.

I hadn't felt that for so long.

I wanted it again. I wanted to *feel* again.

I met Noah's gaze, full of heat, desire, and something stronger, more powerful. Not just lust, but something resembling...awe.

No one had ever looked at me like that. Like I was a magical and beautiful creation.

I didn't just want him to kiss me, I wanted to kiss him. I wanted to taste his lips, feel his mouth on mine. I wanted to explore our connection as far as it would take us.

His hand slid around my jaw, cradling it, coaxing me closer. My eyes closed, and I leaned in.

Ever so slowly, his warm, smooth lips pressed against mine in the gentlest, softest kiss I'd ever had. My body melted into a puddle of bliss. Tiny bolts of lightning zapped through my middle, sparking along my limbs, creating a wild, maddening burst of pleasure.

Wow. If he could do this with the press of his lips, I bet this guy was amazing in bed.

When he hesitated, I moved closer, silently giving him the okay to continue.

His tongue teased along my bottom lip and I barely held back my moan. I parted my lips for him, letting go of any restraint. Not that I had much to begin with.

His free hand cradled the other side of my jaw, tightening his hold, angling my head slightly to deepen the kiss. My shoulders sagged into his embrace, giving in to all the sensations swirling through my body.

For years, I'd lost myself. Lost who I was, what I wanted in life. I lived in the shadow of my mother's poor choices, spending each waking moment gasping for breath.

This kiss breathed life back into my soul. Right here and now, Noah found me.

His grip on my jaw hardened a fraction, not painfully but enough to flip alarm bells. Noah tensed, his lips still touching mine. I opened my eyes. His were bright, alert, side-eyeing the waterfall.

In an instant, he jerked back and slapped a hand over my mouth, pinning my back against the rock.

What the hell? I grabbed his wrist to pull his hand

away, but he applied more pressure. With his free hand, he held his index finger against his lips.

My heart sped for an entirely different reason. Was this some kind of joke?

Noah cocked his ear toward the waterfall as though listening for something I could neither hear nor see. His legs no longer playfully kicking back and forth. Now, his ridged body was alert as though sensing a hidden danger.

He looked back at me. Desire and heat no longer consumed his gaze, instead replaced with cold ice blue, the color so clear his eyes almost glowed in the filtered light.

"Don't make a sound," he whispered.

When I nodded, he lowered his hand. I couldn't move, so frozen with fear of the unknown. What the hell was out there?

As though on cue, through the lens of the waterfall, a shadow stalked along the bank toward our belongings. Tall. Like the size of a bulky male or very well-built female. Maybe the same height as Noah.

Noah said this was his family's land. Why was he hiding from family?

"Who is it?" I whispered.

I doubted someone he didn't know would wander this far onto his property. Unless they meant harm. If that were the case, we were safe, hidden behind the falls. I hoped.

The look in Noah's glare said otherwise. "Shhh."

I glanced back at the shadow. The person paused, then crouched where we left our belongings. Were they looking for something? Shit. My phone was inside my bag. If the guy stole it, I was screwed.

The person stood again. Adrenaline coursed through my body making my stomach twist and swirl until I thought I'd vomit.

Noah squeezed my hand. Some of my tension trickled from me as though a magical link connected us. I wiggled closer.

The weirdo stalked around the bank of the pool. Obviously, searching for the owner of the clothes. I sucked in a sharp breath when they reached the edge of the pool and couldn't go any further without getting into the water.

Did they know we were here? Would they dive in and find us?

Noah's hand tightened around mine. For reassurance or security, I couldn't be sure, but it didn't work.

Then, as quickly as they arrived, the person turned and darted into the forest.

Noah remained still. Waiting to see if the person would reappear? Waiting to know if we were safe?

After an agonizing moment that felt like hours, he pivoted to face me.

"Are you okay?"

Was I okay? How the hell did I answer that? "Who was that?"

Muscles flexed in his jaw. He stared at the waterfall. "A hunter."

chapter eight

Noah

"What the heck?" Mia squawked, her eyes wide. "A hunter? Hunting what?"

She either knew nothing about our world or was a damn good liar. I put all my faith in the former.

I should've left it there, but I couldn't stop the words from spilling out of my mouth. If she didn't know about this world, she needed to. I couldn't lie or hide the truth from her. Not any longer.

I leveled my voice, searching her eyes for a hint she knew, that she was just playing me. I came up empty. "I'll explain everything, but right now we need to get out of here."

She held my stare for a moment before the crease deepened in her forehead. "Is this a joke? 'Cause it's not funny."

"No. It's not a joke. It's real."

"Hunters here in Woodland Falls?"

If we weren't in danger of the hunter returning, I would've breathed a sigh of relief. Based on her reaction, she clearly didn't know.

"Yes. And I need to get you out of here before he comes back."

I didn't give a shit if the hunter came back for me. I counted down the days to that reunion. But I wouldn't put Mia in more danger. I slid off the rock into the water and grabbed her by the hips. "Do you want me to carry you or can you swim back?"

She didn't answer, just kept staring at me. Instead of waiting, I turned around, slid her butt off the ledge and lifted her onto my back. She held on tight as I kept to the shallower edge of the pool, piggybacking her to the bank. When we reached our bags, I unlocked her legs and let them slide for her to stand.

One look at our clothes and my heart sank. The hunter took Mia's shirt. Of course, he did, it had her scent all over it. Fresh meat in Woodland Falls. Only a matter of time before the hunter figured out her connection with Joan, and then with me.

Mia remained silent as I wrapped a towel around her shoulders and helped her put on her shoes. No time to dress, I shoved her shorts in her bag and slung it over my shoulder before picking up my things.

I took her hand, giving it a gentle squeeze. "We're gonna move quickly, 'kay?"

She nodded.

As fast as I could, without revealing my bonus wolf speed, we hurried back to my truck. In an instant, we were driving through the forest toward home.

Bouncing around in the truck, Mia reached for her bag and slipped on her shorts. "I think we left my shirt back there." She searched near her feet and inside her bag again. "I can't find it."

"I'll check later." I wasn't about to tell her a hunter stole it.

Once out of the forest and back in cell reception, I texted Liam to warn him. Yeah, I knew better than texting while driving, but there were times for breaking the rules. This was one of them. I couldn't exactly speak with Mia in earshot.

Instead of texting back, the dumbass called.

I groaned and answered. "Couldn't text?"

"Are you fucking with me?"

"Nope." I accelerated around the bend, dirt and dust filling the rearview mirror.

"Ivy's still here with me. I'll call Ash." Liam paused. "Is Mia with you?"

"Yep."

"Do you think she knows?"

I glanced at Mia in the passenger seat, clutching the seatbelt in one hand. This wasn't how I wanted to tell her. "I hope not."

After ending the call, I tossed the cell on the dash and focused on getting inside the house before the hunter tracked us down. I slammed my foot on the brake, skidding to a halt in front of the porch.

"Why are you stopping here?"

I inhaled a deep breath before pivoting to face Mia. "I want you to stay here tonight with me."

Joan ensured the hunter couldn't sense me at the waterfall, but the psycho took Mia's shirt. By now he could've tracked her scent to the Whitcome property. Then, he'd know who she was.

I doubt he was stupid enough to draw attention in broad daylight. Not after last time. But I wouldn't take the risk.

Mia's brows rose. "That's a bit presumptuous of you, isn't it?"

"No, that's not what I meant. Sure, I wouldn't say no, but that's not why I want you to stay here." Why the hell couldn't I speak properly? I ran my fingers through my hair. "What I mean is, you're safer here."

"From a hunter? Hunting for animals?"

Shifter hunter. But I didn't correct her. I wanted to avoid telling her about the shifter world a little while longer. Discovering shifters existed was one thing. But finding out we both shared that world was a whole other complication.

Mia exhaled a deep sigh. "Noah, I've known you for less than two weeks. I appreciate you feeling the need to protect me, it's sweet, but I feel totally safe at my house. There's no need to worry about a guy hunting some animal busting down my door."

I needed to approach this from a different angle, rather than the creepy guy who wanted in her pants. Which I wouldn't mind, but again, that wasn't the point.

"It's just a shame to have our afternoon cut short like that."

Damn it. That sounded creepier aloud than it did in my head.

Her eyes narrowed. She wasn't stupid. Of course, she wasn't, she's my mate. Will be. At some point. *Ugh.*

She straightened in her seat. "Actually, I have a few things I need to do this afternoon."

I wouldn't pressure her into staying and I sure as hell wouldn't force her. If she wanted to go home, then I'd take her. Instead of protecting her at my house, I'd change tactics and shift, so I could watch over her from the forest.

The hunter was after me, not her. But if that psycho joined the dots and linked Mia to Joan, she could end up hurt. Or worse.

Just like Joan.

I tightened my grip on the steering wheel. Why was the universe so fucking twisted? I needed to keep her close to ensure her safety, yet, I needed to keep my distance to make sure the hunter didn't figure out she was mine.

If Mia already knew? It didn't matter. As her mate, I would still protect her for life.

"You're right." I swallowed the lump in my throat and put the truck in gear. "I'll take you home."

Mia

I collapsed in the chair on the back porch facing the forest. What a day. I doubt it could've gotten any weirder. Noah kissed me and then some random hunter rummaged through my things. He probably stole my shirt like some pervert.

Bears didn't inhabit this part of Montana that I knew of, so why would hunters come here? Unless they hunted protected animals, like wolves. Not only was that illegal, I also hadn't seen any wolves since I'd come back.

Regardless, the day was beyond weird, creepy even, and I hadn't heard from Noah the rest of the afternoon.

As dusk settled behind the forest, I flipped on the porch lights and grabbed my sketch book and pencil. Even as an adult, staring at the forest behind Joan's place was one of my favorite places. I'd forgotten how much I loved it. Towering trees, the crisp scent of pine needles lingering in the air, the mysterious treasures I imagined hid amongst the branches. The peacefulness. In winter, dusted in snow, this place would be breathtaking.

Wait up. Just because I loved the view, coupled with one spectacular kiss from Noah, didn't mean I'd stay here. Though, part of me effortlessly envisioned a future in this house. I didn't have much of a life back in Seattle anyway. I'd already lost my job because I embarked on an eight-week vacation and by the end of the summer, I would've burned through my savings just to pay my half of the rent on my shared apartment. Packing up and starting a new life here seemed like the logical option.

I exhaled a long breath. I'd consider those big decisions tomorrow. Tonight, I had the urge to sketch. I hardly made the time back in Seattle. Even before I finished college, I worked fulltime and barely had time for anything else. Art didn't pay as well as people imagined.

I dragged the chair to the right, stopping at the top of the stairs for an uninterrupted view of the forest. Deep orange shone between the branches, darkening as the minutes ticked by. I held the pencil between my fingers and let go. With each stroke, the tension and weirdness from the day drifted into the background.

Daylight faded, replaced by the porch lights spilling over the lawn, but my pencil never stilled, pouring emotion, and longing onto the page. It reminded me of the last time I came here, where I sat on the grass each afternoon filling the pages with black and white sketches of my wolf friend.

A branch snapped at the far corner of the yard. My pencil stilled along with my breath. I waited, listened. When I heard nothing else, I resumed sketching. Clearly, I was still a little jumpy given what happened at the waterfall. I probably imagined it.

Focusing back on the page, I shaded the trunk of one tree, rubbing it with my thumb to smudge the pencil and create depth in the bark.

Another branch snapped. Closer this time. Nope, I didn't imagine it.

A squirrel probably rummaging for food. Still, I paused again, straining to identify what made the noise. My ears buzzed in the silence. A weird sensation tugged at my chest like a fist squeezing and pulling at my heart.

I placed the sketch pad and pencil on the table and

stood at the top of the stairs, scanning the yard. Nothing... My breath hitched. At the far end, surrounded by darkness and almost completely hidden between the trees, a set of ice-blue eyes stared back at me.

I'd know those eyes anywhere. *My wolf.*

"Thor," I whispered. The name I gave him for his protection, bravery, and strength. In one summer, he healed the heart I hadn't known was broken.

But how was Thor still here fifteen years later? I thought wolves lived for only five or so years. I descended the stairs quietly and slowly, so I didn't spook him. Would he recognize my scent? Would he trust me?

I inched closer.

Thor whined and retreated a step, almost hesitant for me to approach. I stilled. Maybe this wasn't him. Maybe this wolf was related to mine, which explained why the eyes were the same shade? A pup or more likely its pup's pup?

No. Even knowing the unlikely odds, that tugging in my chest told me this wolf was my Thor. My heart squeezed. Fifteen years ago, he was the only thing that got me through the summer. Our unconventional friendship made me feel safe, protected, loved. Whole.

I'd give anything to feel that again.

Slow and steady, I crept closer, my palm held out in front of me.

This time, Thor's whine morphed into a low rumble. A warning. But he didn't retreat.

A few feet away, I crouched on the dewy grass. Just like the first time we met, I ventured halfway. Now it was his turn. I hoped he recognized me as I did him. Though, even if he didn't, I'd be content sitting here at a distance admiring his glossy black fur. I wished I'd brought my sketch pad. I considered darting back for it, but with my luck the sudden movement would scare him, and he'd bolt into the forest.

One black front paw moved forward, stepping from the tree line. I held my breath. Thor's gaze met mine. Recognition tickled the back of my mind. Those eyes. I'd seen them before, not just on him, but somewhere more recent. Where?

When I sensed he wanted to come closer, I held out my open hand. "Come here, Thor."

Silently, he drew nearer. My heart pounded behind my ribs.

As soon as he was within reach, Thor lowered his head and whined. A sound so familiar, it resonated through my blood, curling around my heart. That tugging sensation intensified.

I reached out and smoothed my fingers through the bristly, black fur at his neck. Thor leaned into my touch.

"I've missed you. So much," I whispered.

A sense of belonging spread through my chest, right to the center of my soul. My shoulders sagged under the weight of all the decisions I'd made leading me to this moment. Why did I stay away from here? I could've come back to Woodland Falls whenever I wanted. Joan would've welcomed me with open arms. Instead, I avoided it. Why?

Fear of failure? Disappointment? I didn't know. Until Joan, the only family I ever loved did nothing for me in return. I hated the thought of becoming my mother, but even more so, it scared me to want something more from Joan. Instead, I made do with the memories of how perfect that one summer was until my mother returned and took it all away.

Joan must've known. Otherwise, why else would she include the condition in her will? She wanted me to not just find peace here, but find myself, discover who I truly was out from under the dark shadow of my mother.

Not that I'd seen my mother in what felt like forever. I didn't even know where she was these days. She'd never bothered to track me down once I left.

Thor nuzzled my face, licking my cheek, bringing me back to the present. I giggled, really giggled for the first time in ages. I'd missed this. Until this moment, I hadn't realized how much.

"I can't believe it's you. How is this possible?"

I scratched him behind the ears in the exact spot he used to love.

"Have you waited for me this whole time?" Pressure caved in on my ribs. "I'm sorry I left. I didn't even say goodbye."

Unshed tears burned in my eyes. Thor whined again, as though sensing the shift in my mood.

I smiled. Wolves were such sensitive and beautiful creatures. Noah was right about that.

"Did you find your mate?"

He licked my cheek again. I sank back on my haunches, and Thor placed his paw on my knee.

I'd never seen other wolves in the forest. Noah said they valued family above everything else, but what happened when they didn't belong to a pack? They became the lone wolf. Just like Noah's tattoo.

Just like me.

"Are you a lone wolf, Thor? Is that why we're such good friends?" I ruffled the fur at his neck again. "It's okay. We can be our own pack and wander the earth together."

Thor stilled and cocked his head to one side.

Noah had moved in a similar way when the hunter—

A low growl rumbled deep inside Thor's chest. A warning, loud and clear. Did he sense a threat? His lips curled back in a snarl, revealing sharp fangs. I jerked backward, even though I knew he didn't aim his aggression at me. Thor spun, growling at the trees. Something else was out there.

Thor turned to me, snapping his jaw, forcing me backward. I scrambled to stand. He kept snapping until I backed all the way up the stairs onto the porch. He paused, two front paws on the bottom step, growling at me.

"Okay, I get the hint. Playtime is over."

For some reason, Thor wanted me inside the house. Now.

I grabbed my sketch pad and pencil, and dashed inside, locking the door behind me. My pulse raced. Was a hunter in the forest? If so, why was Thor so concerned with my safety and not his own?

From behind the kitchen window, I watched him dart toward the forest. Just before he entered, he peered back at me for a split second then bolted into the darkness.

chapter nine

Noah

I came to buck-naked on all fours just beyond the edge of the forest. I rolled my neck loosening the muscles. A sweet after-shift burn spread through my limbs, made worse by how far my wolf had run. But I couldn't rest. I needed to get to Mia and make sure she was safe.

I stood, grabbed the pile of clothes I left by a tree and shoved on my jeans and shoes. Racing out of the forest, I pulled a shirt over my head and ran straight up the front steps and into the Cole house.

After my call earlier in the day, Liam closed the bar

and bunkered down with Ivy inside the house. To a hunter, an ordinary human family lived on the farm.

Large packs worked together to take down hunters. We were a tiny pack of four with only three shifters. This hunter wouldn't stop until he discovered our location and got what he came for—blood.

The second I returned from Mia's, Ash shifted with me and joined the hunt. We became the hunters instead of the hunted. But we'd lost the hunter's trail to the far west of the forest near the main road leading to Timber Falls. That asshole had been at Mia's place, I smelled his retched scent all over the lawn but thank fuck he didn't stick around.

The hunter had clearly picked up a few tricks since our last encounter.

By the hall table, I paused and inhaled a deep breath filled with Mia's jasmine scent. It coated my body like an extra skin. Even though I'd shifted with a single intention to remain in the forest, my damn wolf didn't listen and stepped onto the lawn.

I envied it. To have a connection with her without secrets or expectations or having to deal with all the shit that came with being in human form.

Enough was enough. She clearly didn't know about this world. She needed to realize the dangers and that no matter which path she chose, I'd protect her. I'd sat on the sidelines for fifteen fucking years. I wouldn't do it any longer, especially while Mia remained in that house unaware.

The hunter might not attack her place right away, but it wouldn't be long until that psycho figured out she was a

Whitcome descendant. Then he'd know her link with me. I wouldn't sit on my ass while the hunter planned his next move. Been there, done that. And Joan died because of my negligence.

I wouldn't make that mistake again.

I snatched my cell and keys from the side table. Four missed calls from Mia. I didn't need to listen to the messages to know they were about my wolf and what just happened in her backyard. I retained that memory after I shifted back.

Now she needed to know her wolf and I were one and the same.

Liam walked around the corner into the hall. "Kill that sonofabitch yet?"

"Working on it." Fury clenched my jaw. "Ash and I lost the scent."

The front door slammed opened, and Ash strode in, shirt hanging from his hands. "I doubled back in case we missed something. We didn't."

"I lost the trail near the Henderson property. He might be heading to Timber Falls."

Liam pulled out his cell, thumbing the screen. "I'll let Baker know, so he can be on alert if the hunter shows up there."

"Good idea." Ash slipped on his shirt. "We'll get him, Noah."

I wasn't so sure. Once maybe, but that psycho had terrorized us for long enough. This needed to end before someone else died.

"I'm going to Mia." A whole lot of silence from Ash and Liam. "I can't keep tiptoeing around this. She's safer knowing. And if I go to her, I can be on the front foot if she already knows."

Ash nodded. "I agree."

Wait. "You do?"

"This hunter isn't going to stop. Leaving her unprotected at that house isn't wise. Especially after..."

Joan.

I'd never admit it aloud, but Ash's support meant more to me than he realized. With less than two years between us, I still looked up to him. Even more after Dad passed.

He gripped my shoulder giving it a firm squeeze. "Let me know how it goes. I'll text you once we hear from Baker."

"Will do."

At the door, I paused and turned back. "Ash?"

"Yeah?"

"Thanks, man. I mean it."

A soft smile hinted on Ash's face. "I think Mom would've loved Mia."

My eyes stung. "Me, too."

Before I got all sappy, I tucked the cell in my jeans and left, jogging down the stairs to my truck.

I sped down the road, ignoring the speed limit.

Once in Mia's drive, I sat there for a moment while my heart stopped launching from my chest. For fifteen years, I dreamed of telling her. And now that hunter forced my hand. I would've told her eventually, I just wished it were under better circumstances.

I took the key from the ignition and got out of the truck. I still couldn't believe I kissed her today. I hadn't planned to, it just happened. The stars aligned, so I seized that moment with both hands. And it was fucking worth it. Everything I'd hoped it would be and more. The mate connection between us zapped through my blood, racing around my body. I sensed she felt it too by the way her eyes flew open with a gasp.

Hopefully, she recalled our connection when I showed her who I really was. She already knew my wolf, and soon she'd know the real me. After that, I'd tell her everything. The night would end in one of two ways: an unbreakable bond or my ass out on the street.

Of course, I hoped for the former. I'd waited fifteen years to tell her how I felt, to show her my true self. Surely, it was about time the universe cut me some slack.

As I strode to the porch, I inhaled a deep breath, sifting through the scents in the night air, searching for the hunter. He wasn't here. Time might be on our side for once.

My heart wouldn't calm the fuck down. Her laugh, her smile, the way she looked at me like she knew. Not just that she was my mate, but I sensed deep down she knew about me. My wolf. Even if she didn't admit it to herself, once she saw my eyes tonight, she'd piece it all together.

When I reached the veranda, Mia flung open the door, her eyes wide and frantic. "I left you like a thousand messages."

"I know." Reaching her, I cupped her cheeks between my hands. "Are you okay?"

Jesus. My scent was all over her. My damn wolf must've licked her entire face. Bastard.

She relaxed in my embrace and exhaled a long breath. "Yes. No. I don't know. I'm kind of freaked out."

I bent so we were eye level. "I'm here."

Her brows pinched as she stared into my eyes, but she didn't say anything.

"May I come in?"

She nodded. I lowered my hands, following her inside, locking the door behind me. That wouldn't stop the hunter. That psycho would blow up the joint to get to me. Or another Whitcome.

I followed Mia into the kitchen. She leaned against the counter while I stood there all awkward, hands shoved in my jean pockets.

"I think someone was here tonight, in the forest. Noah, what the hell is going on?"

"There's a hunter in Woodland Falls. The guy is dangerous."

She tilted her head slightly, studying me. "I didn't think hunters came here. Even if they did, why would they hurt people?"

My pulse raced, and my wolf paced back and forth ready to take over. *Calm the fuck down. This is my time.* I sent the mental command, but the stubborn bastard didn't obey as usual.

This conversation was harder than I expected.

I dragged a chair from the dining table, but before I sat, a picture frame hanging on the living room wall caught my attention. I gravitated to it. Encased in a simple thin wooden frame was a black and white sketch of a wolf in a yard. I recognized it immediately. The tool shed of horrors at the far side, the empty vegetable patch, the tire swing hanging from a tree. Pressure squeezed my chest as I brushed my finger along the frame. This sketch was the first time Mia met me in wolf form. The moment I found my mate.

Mia came up beside me.

I turned to her. "Who drew this?"

Light pink bloomed over her cheeks. "Me. I like to sketch." Without taking her gaze off the drawing, a soft smile lifted on her lips. "I came here one summer. My mother dumped me with Joan because she had better things to do. It was the first time I met my grandma and the only time I spent with her."

She paused. I held my breath waiting for her to say it. *Wanting* her to say it.

"I befriended a wolf. It wandered out of the forest the first day I arrived, and every afternoon after. Thick black fur, long nose." Her smile widened. "He had this one brindle patch on his chest. And the most haunting ice-blue eyes."

Her palm rested on her chest, in the spot where my wolf had the brindle patch.

A tremor quaked low in my gut. I clenched my jaw, sending the impatient bastard a silent message to wait his turn. Or maybe it was my way of delaying the shift. I mean, I wanted to show her, I needed to, but...*shit*. What if she freaked out? What if she hated me for not telling her earlier?

What if she resented me for what happened with Joan?

She turned to face me and laughed. "Sounds silly, I know, but I swear that same wolf was here in the yard tonight. It growled at me until I hurried back inside the house." She looked at the sketch.

My heart thumped so hard it made me want to vomit. I slid my hand in hers, lacing our fingers together. "It's not silly."

"Over the years, I often wondered what happened to him. I left so suddenly. Did he sit in the yard waiting for me to come back? Did Joan shoo him away or scare him with her shotgun."

I returned every afternoon in wolf form and waited for her. For goddamn years. Joan sat on the back porch in an unspoken truce. Then one day, she told me the girl wasn't coming back. So, neither did I.

My chest squeezed tighter. Joan wasn't like the others. I hoped Mia wasn't either.

Now was my opportunity, the most perfect segue to tell her about me. If I shut this down and didn't answer, I may not get another. I needed to go for it. To man up and tell her.

I stared at our joined hands, amazed at how naturally they fit together while I considered my words. I didn't want to come across too eager and blurt it all out at once. Where was the manual for this? Liam told Ivy when they were kids. Kids accepted anything, without judgement or bias. Adults? Not so much.

I lifted my gaze to hers. "The wolves in the woods behind your house have been there for generations."

She frowned. "But it can't be the same one. I didn't think they lived that long."

"Once they reach adulthood, they age slower."

Shifters, not ordinary wolves.

Her eyes narrowed. "But slow enough to still be here fifteen years later?"

I nodded, 'cause words were a little hard right now.

"I've only ever seen one here." She peered through the kitchen, in the direction of the forest. "I wonder if he ever found his mate."

"He did."

My breath stalled. I didn't mean to say that aloud.

"How do you know?"

Another tremor quaked in my gut, harder this time. My wolf was an impatient bastard. He wanted to show Mia too, I knew that. Showing her was the only way to prove it beyond a doubt.

I hoped she didn't freak out when she discovered the wolf she befriended all those years ago, the one that shouldered her pain every day, was the same man she'd gotten to know over the past fortnight. The man who loved her from the moment he first saw her in that window fifteen years ago and pined for her every day after she left.

I squeezed her hand. Now or never. "I want to show you something, but I need you to keep an open mind."

"Okaaay."

Still holding her hand, I led her out to the back porch and flipped on the light. Shifting inside the house never ended well, wolves had a tendency to break shit. Plus, if Mia freaked out, I didn't want her to feel like she had no safe place to retreat.

At the top of the stairs, I let her hand slip from mine as I descended onto the lawn. She held back.

I swallowed, trying to clear the big lump parked in my throat. "Close your eyes. Picture your wolf."

Your wolf. That sounded so goddamn good.

She gasped, eyes darting to the far end of the yard. "Is he here? Do you see him?"

My pulse wouldn't let up. "Close your eyes."

She didn't.

I really didn't want to shift while she watched. Not everyone took that well. Though, Liam did that with Ivy. But again, kids. This was different. If Mia left town again, I sensed she'd never come back. I'd never mate. I'd become the lone wolf I always feared.

Shifting in front of her was a huge gamble. If she wasn't like Joan...

I lowered my voice. "It's okay. Close your eyes."

Her gaze drifted between me and the forest before her eyes slid closed.

I didn't waste any time. The last thing I wanted was for her to open her eyes mid-shift and freak out. If this went well, we had years for her to watch me shift. First, I needed this gamble to pay off.

I stripped off my shirt and dropped it on the grass.

Mia peeked open one eye.

"No cheating."

"If you're planning to get naked, you can do that inside the house you know." Her lips thinned. "I get the feeling it's not safe out here."

Striding up the steps, I halted one step below her, so we were both eye level. Leaning in, I brushed my knuckles along her smooth jaw. "You're safe with me."

I eased my mouth against hers and kissed her. Slow,

gentle, and deep. A kiss I hoped told her we belonged together, that I'd waited for her. That I would wait another lifetime if it meant making her mine. Before I forgot why the hell I took off my shirt, I eased back and returned to the lawn. Mia kept her eyes closed.

Tremors rumbled through my body and my blood heated. In case Mia opened her eyes again, I quickly stripped off the rest of my clothes and tossed them on the ground. My wolf paced back and forth, gearing up for the shift.

This time I let it take control. Closing my eyes, I handed over the reins. Heat erupted down my spine, flaring through my blood. Quakes raged in every cell as I shifted in one swift motion.

For a split second, through the sharp, tinted lens of my wolf, I saw Mia staring, wide-eyed before my mind blacked out.

chapter ten

Mia

I shouldn't have peeked. I should've kept my eyes closed, but my pounding heart nearly made me dizzy. Noah acted so strange, and coupled with Thor's behavior earlier, I wasn't in the mood for surprises. My mother excelled at delivering them throughout my childhood. Never good ones.

As I peeked, I watched him toss his clothes on the grass until he stood there naked. Completely naked. But before I had the chance to drool over all those muscles covered in ink, the air around his shoulders shifted, vibrations pulsed in the air. His head lowered as his shoulders twitched, his breathing became louder, transforming into a low rumbly growl.

My heart soared. I knew that growl.

Hang on. That growl didn't come from my wolf. It came from...Noah.

His body jolted, he keeled over at the waist and—

In one swift movement, Noah transformed into a wolf.

My eyes flung wide and I slapped a hand over my mouth holding back a scream. *What the hell?*

Dizziness threatened to topple me as I gaped at the large black wolf on the lawn where Noah stood only a second ago. Recognition pushed through before panic took hold. Those eyes. The brindle patch on the wolf's chest. The growl I heard.

That wasn't just any wolf.

Thor.

Gripping the banister for support, I crept down the stairs, but at the bottom, my legs gave way and I collapsed onto the step. My heart raced, nearly exploding from my chest. How did that happen? How was Noah, the guy I met in the bar last week, the same wolf I befriended fifteen years ago?

How was this possible?

Did my grandma know? Was this why she wanted me to stay here for the summer?

Thor lowered his nose to the grass and whined. Just like he did earlier tonight.

Oh, my Lord. This explained why I sensed a connection with Noah from the moment I saw him. We had met before, just not in person.

I held out my hand and Thor padded closer, licking the inside of my palm.

Once the adrenaline faded, a crazed giggle rose in my chest until it burst from me. I laughed so hard tears trickled down my cheeks. All this time, I thought a wolf was the only living creature who ever understood me. Turned out, that wolf was actually a freaking hot guy.

I raked my fingers through the fur behind Thor's ear. Once again, I couldn't wipe the smile from my face.

"I can't believe you're an actual person."

He lowered his head and leaned into my touch.

As much as I wanted to sit here with Thor, I needed to talk about this. So many questions raced around in my head. Some made me giddy, others caused a knot to form low in my belly. Now I knew what animal the hunter hunted.

"Can you, you know, change back so I can talk to you?"

The wolf whined again and angled his head for a better scratch.

"Please?" I gave him an extra good scratch behind the ears. "I really need to talk to you. Not that I don't enjoying petting you as a wolf." *Okay, that sounded so weird.* "But as a wolf you can't exactly answer my questions."

He straightened, looked at me, then moved back to put some space between us. I stood, holding the banister for support.

Like before, the air around the wolf rippled, his head shook left and right, shoulders rolled inward. In one swift movement, beast turned into man and Noah was on all fours buck-naked.

"Noah," I whispered.

He stood. My pulse raced. Not just because a gorgeous guy stood naked in my yard, but because I knew him. I'd always known him. I stared into the familiar blue eyes as all the pieces clicked into place. Why hadn't I noticed the similarities in their eyes?

"Are you okay?" Concern etched his face, deep grooves in his forehead.

I couldn't stop smiling. I mean, I should be freaking out right now. The wolf I befriended as a teen and the gorgeous guy I met at a bar were one and the same. Was that so farfetched to believe? *Kinda.* Though it certainly explained why hanging out with Noah seemed so easy and natural as though we'd done it many times before. Because we had.

Besides, Noah secretly being a wolf was pretty damn cool.

I smiled up at Noah trying to reassure him. He looked a heck of a lot more freaked out than me. "That was, hands down, the most amazing thing I've ever seen."

His shoulder slumped with a heavy exhaled. "I've been wanting to tell you, but it was never the right time."

He acted totally at home standing naked in my back-yard. Maybe it was a wolf thing? Either way, having all that golden-tanned flesh within arm's reach sent tiny shivers dancing through my middle, centering between my legs.

It'd been a long time since I saw a man naked. Even longer, if ever, since I truly appreciated the view. My breath quickened. He either needed to dress, or I needed to step back and put some space between us.

I swallowed. "And now's the right time?"

He closed the distance. His body heat coupled with his wild and earthy scent, surrounded me making my head swim.

"I hope so. 'Cause I've waited fifteen years to show you the real me and I don't wanna screw this up."

My breath caught somewhere in my chest. "You've waited this whole time to show me?"

He drew even closer, until only a sliver of space remained between us. I became increasingly aware of his nakedness. Not in a weird way. In a way that awakened every cell in my body.

He cupped my jaw, smoothing his thumb along my cheek. Again, the touch seemed so familiar.

"I haven't just waited to show you. I've waited *for* you."

And there went my heart, flipping upside down and inside out.

I was right. This guy could convince me to pack up my life in Seattle and stay here in the middle of nowhere. Fifteen years ago, I wanted to run away with Thor and live in the forest forever. Less than an hour ago, I told him we'd wander the earth together, never alone.

The last piece of the puzzle fell into place. Thor hadn't found his wolf mate. Man and wolf had waited for me.

I flattened my palm over Noah's thumping heart. It beat loud and strong, like him and his beast were one.

"I'm...your mate." I whispered the words, still unsure I comprehended their meaning.

Did I imagine our connection? Was the story he told true? Did wolves wait forever for their mate?

My breath hitched. Did the lone wolf on his wrist represent him?

"Yes." He held my face in his strong hands, searching my eyes.

The world vanished.

"That summer when you first came here, I sensed you in the forest and tracked your scent all the way to Joan's house. I found you staring out that window. I knew the second I saw you. But I had to make sure it was safe." His lips rolled inward. "Tell me you feel the bond between us."

Did I? I sensed a connection with Thor, the tug that drew me to the window when I first arrived. That same connection lured me to the yard every afternoon, desperate to see the wolf. I thought back to when I arrived at the bar, where a similar, if not the same, pull drew me to Noah. A spark had zapped through my middle the moment our gazes collided. Not a love at first sight spark, but something stronger, deeper. Ancient.

I joked that we'd known each other in a past life, but this explained it. A higher power connected the two of us as though we were destined for each other.

"I do."

I guess that was the right answer. The second the words were out Noah took my mouth with his. Hot, hungry, and raw. A kiss that wasn't just the meeting of two mouths, but two souls finding each other after a lifetime apart. Yearning, need, and desire swirled together in one tumbling mess. Noah angled my head to deepen the kiss, drawing a soft moan from my lips.

I embraced our connection, every sensation overtaking my body until it left me aching for more. Knowing what he was, that he stepped into my life so long ago, felt like I'd finally come home. No, not came home, found home.

Noah was my home.

He slowed the kiss before easing back, but kept his hands around my face, lowering his forehead to mine. Glorious sensations trickled through my body as a sweet ache built between my legs.

"I don't want to rush this," he whispered.

That made me smirk. "You call waiting fifteen years rushing?"

"You know what I mean." He kissed me again, a soft peck on my forehead. "We should talk first. There are things I need to tell you before we go any further."

I ran my fingers down his sides, grazing my nails along his waist, halting at his hips. His erection thickened between us, pressing against my lower belly. I figured I had two choices. I could step back, let him put his clothes on and we could go inside to talk. Or I could surrender to the intensity between us and see where it led.

We only just met in person, but we'd known each other for what felt like a lifetime. We had plenty of time to talk later.

I lifted my gaze to meet those glacier pools of blue. "The second I saw you in the bar, I felt like we'd met before. I sensed this connection between us." I slid my hands around to his lower back. "I thought at first maybe we'd known each other in a past life, but that sounded too crazy. Turns out, the real reason was even more unbelievable."

His lips kicked up on one side, and that dimple deepened, making my legs weak.

"I have lots of questions, but right now, I..."

He curled a finger under my chin, lifting my gaze back to his. "You what?"

"I feel like I was meant to come back here. I was meant to see you again." I traced his firm, rigid abs, sliding my hands up to his chest. "I was meant to be with you."

Noah held my gaze for what seemed like forever, searching for something. A second, a minute, I couldn't tell. Whatever he looked for, he must've found it because his hands guided my face to his and he kissed me.

My world spun, blurring in a fierce collision of emotion. Longing, lust, and something else clenched my heart. I didn't even flinch when he lifted me, locking my legs around his waist, and carried me up the stairs and inside the house. He paused for a moment, as though deciding which direction.

"Couch?" I murmured between kisses.

I had no doubt he could carry me up the stairs to my bedroom, but I was too impatient to wait.

Still kissing me, he instead diverted to the nearby kitchen, lowering my butt onto the counter. Positioned between my legs, he trailed hot kisses down my neck as his hands slipped under my shirt. Every cell in my body sizzled, his fingers leaving a white-hot trail over my skin.

Up went my arms and off came my shirt. He threw it behind him somewhere. He kissed me again, harder this time. Gripping my butt, he lifted me off the counter and lowered my legs to stand. He dragged down my sweatpants and I kicked them off my feet.

I panted like crazy, standing before him in just my underwear. In hindsight, I should've worn prettier ones.

"You're so beautiful," he murmured, tracing a finger between my breasts.

His thumb brushed over the fabric of my bra sending a wild burst of heat to my core. He kissed along my collarbone, dragging my bra strap down as his mouth trailed across my shoulder. In one impressive move, he unclasped and slipped off my bra, before continuing his kisses down my chest to my breasts.

Before, when I said I couldn't remember ever taking the time to admire a guy's naked body, I also couldn't remember a guy ever admiring mine like Noah did now. His molten gaze tracked along every inch of my skin, not just with lust, but with hunger, desire, and that look he'd given me earlier. Awe.

My lower back pressed into the countertop, my breathing heavy. Noah was magnificent. Smooth golden skin, perfectly defined muscles. The tattoos along his torso came alive with every flex. My head fell back as his mouth continued exploring. He worshipped my body with kisses and soft gentle strokes, sending a wild burst of fire through my blood.

His hands trailed down my stomach, hooking his fingers beneath the waist of my panties. Slowly, he dragged them down, planting sweet kisses along my middle.

As he straightened, he slid his hand up the inside of my thighs, brushing the apex. The possessive look in his gaze almost undid me. I wanted him to not just touch me but devour me. Make me his forever.

He gripped my hips and lifted me back onto the counter. With one hand on my belly, he gently coaxed me onto my back.

His gaze dipped to my core. "I've waited so long to make you mine."

Oh, hell. If his mouth ventured anywhere near down there, I'd fall apart and never recover.

I held my breath, the anticipation a sweet sinful torture. The moment his tongue lapped my core, I all but exploded. My lower back arched off the counter.

His tongue circled, and stroked, building me higher and higher. My fingers curled on the countertop, searching for something to grip but coming up empty. Just when I thought I couldn't stand it any longer, Noah caught me between his lips, and I flew off the cliff. Glittering lights burst before my eyes. Heat flashed through every vein in my body.

Delicate kisses traveled the inside of my thigh, working their way up to my middle as tiny tremors erupted over my skin. When he straightened, he curled an arm around my back and lifted me upright, holding me against him.

I moaned as delicious shivers danced along my spine.

Noah swept hair back from my face and kissed me. I rocked my hips, trying to increase the friction as the ache built once again. His fingers dug into my butt cheeks, pressing me harder against him.

"Condom?" I panted.

He cursed. "My wallet's in my jeans." He stepped back, his breath fast and hard. "Maybe we should slow down. Talk first."

"For real? You're not leaving me hanging like this." I shooed him. "Go. We'll talk later."

His brows furrowed. "Don't leave."

"Why would I leave?"

He held my stare for a moment. Loss and pain flashed across his face. I'd unintentionally left him once before, without warning, and he'd waited fifteen years for me to come back.

I placed my hand on his chest right above his thumping heart. "I'm not going anywhere."

"Good. 'Cause I'm never letting you go."

In less time than humanly possible, Noah dashed outside and returned with his pile of clothes. He grabbed a condom from his wallet and tossed the jeans on the floor.

Back between my legs, he gave my butt a playful squeeze. "Now, where were we?"

"You were kissing me."

"Hmm, that sounds right." His mouth trailed down my neck, while one hand rolled and pinched my nipple. The ache between my legs soared to even higher heights.

I moaned as my limbs became jelly. His arm snaked around my lower back, holding me closer to him. Tingles burned and ached. My insides twisted and clenched, building to that glorious place just out of reach.

He broke our kiss to rip open the condom packet with his teeth and cover himself. He took my mouth again, wrapped his arm around my waist and lifted me off the counter. In a few long strides, he lay me lengthways on the couch beneath him. Lifting one of my legs, he eased inside me. My world shattered. I didn't know much about shifters or destined mates, but if it felt like this, I'd die happy and complete.

Noah gently rocked. An intensity I'd never experienced slowly built from within, higher and higher I climbed until I teetered on the edge of another release. I locked my other leg around his lower back, changing the angle. A delicious burn spread through my blood and I closed my eyes, losing myself in all the sensations.

"Open your eyes, baby."

They fluttered open. His gaze locked with mine, and the possessiveness undid me.

"I want you to see me claim you."

Claim me? Need and desire took over and I didn't bother questioning his choice of words.

I couldn't deny our connection any longer, and in that moment, I surrendered to it. I gave into every sensation swirling through my body into one giant collision. As though sensing my release, Noah reached his hand between us. I cried out. Fireworks exploded before my eyes as I flew over the edge so hard and fast, I almost blacked out. Heat flashed across my skin, and something deep inside me shattered into a million pieces.

Noah increased the pace, fingers digging into my hips holding me in place. My back rubbed along the couch fabric. I'd probably have a burn there tomorrow, but I didn't care. He bent down, pressing his weight on top of mine, taking my mouth in his. His tongue caressed mine as his powerful body shuddered and a low growl rumbled from his chest.

His lips trailed down my jaw to my neck. The second his teeth grazed the sensitive skin at the base of my neck, I checked out, flying over the edge again, this time with him. One word flashed over and over in my mind: *Mine.*

I didn't know how long we lay there while our breathing steadied. Noah buried his face in the crook of my neck, gently grazing his fingers up and down my side while the tremors faded. My leg slid from behind his back to dangle over the side of the couch.

Every muscle in my entire body was utterly spent. This right here was everything I didn't know I wanted.

chapter eleven

Noah

I snuggled on the couch with Mia wrapped between my arms and a blanket draped over our naked bodies. I hadn't meant to mate with her, but it seemed so right. All those glittery stars and far away worlds had aligned once again, so I ran with it. Then why the hell was there a dull ache in my chest? As right as being with her felt, I should've told her about the mating bond before we had sex. Just as I divulged one secret, I gained another.

Mia rolled over in my embrace to lay on her side facing me. Her eyelids heavy, cheeks dusted with a light shade of pink, lips looking as though I'd thoroughly devoured them. Which I had. She was so damn beautiful I didn't know what I'd done to deserve her.

I should probably take her to bed rather than squishing together on the couch.

"So...you're Thor," she murmured, tracing her finger along my arm.

I snorted. "Thor? For my god-like...hammer?"

"No." She chuckled and playfully swatted my shoulder. "I named the wolf version of you Thor because he was so protective of me, turning up at the same time each day, never letting me wander in the forest alone. He was always one step behind me."

Could this woman be any more perfect?

"He'll always protect you." I brushed a lose strand of hair behind her ear. "We both will."

A smile warmed her face. "Are your brothers wolves, too?"

"Shifters. We can shift between wolf and human form. The Coles are the only shifter family here in Woodland Falls."

My shoulders lightened telling her about the shifter world, being honest for once and not hiding behind a human mask. I envied Liam telling Ivy when they were so young. They had all that time together without secrets. Mia and I had just met in person, so I guessed this was the start of our lives together.

Would it have been harder if I told her fifteen years ago, only to have her leave? *Absolutely.*

She drew soft circles on my chest. "Are there other animals or just wolves?"

I thought for a moment. How much should I tell her?

She seemed to take all of this in her stride. Given her reaction on the lawn she clearly knew little, if anything, about this world.

"There are plenty of different shifters out there. A bear pack lives in Cedar Valley, plus there's another wolf pack in Timber Falls."

Dad believed the universe matched shifters with not just their equal, but someone who made them stronger. I witnessed that with Mom and Dad, also with Liam. I'd always joked that Ivy had more bite than him. Being with Mia made me feel exactly that. Stronger. Complete. Worthy of a life with her.

Mia held the key to my soul, but she also possessed an unearthly amount of courage. To be a Whitcome and still choose me. Not everyone would do that. An invisible thread stirred deep inside my soul, connecting us. An unbreakable bond that now tied us together for the rest of our lives.

"The hunter hunts wolves. That's why you're so concerned."

I wriggled my arm out from underneath her to prop up my head. "How much do you know about Joan?"

"I hardly knew her. I came here once when I was fourteen, and then never saw her again."

Her gaze grew distant, tracking her finger as it trailed along the lines of the ink over my chest.

"I wish I'd known her better. She obviously cared for me. I mean, she left me all this."

Maybe there was hope after all.

"Why do the hunters hunt wolves? Do they know you're an actual person?"

I swallowed, not liking where this conversation headed but I didn't want to lie to her any longer. I didn't want more secrets between us. "Hunters are born human but with a dormant curse."

"A curse? As in from a spell?"

I nodded. "Some say it dates to an ancient war between witches and shifters, where a powerful witch performed a blood ritual to annihilate all shifters. But it backfired when she turned herself and her entire coven into hunters. Now, the hunter curse is passed down to every descendant."

"Oh my god," she whispered. "Wolves, witches and hunters. An entire world I knew nothing about." She thought for a moment. "How is the curse triggered in the hunters?" She paused, screwing up her face. "Or do I not want to know?"

I clenched my jaw. Even though she barely knew Joan, it still made me uneasy introducing her to this world. What if I planted ideas in her head? But I had to trust she was different.

Mia was now officially my mate. That had to count for something.

"Blood. The curse compels the hunter to not just kill shifters but drink the blood. Although the compulsion is weaker while the curse is dormant. The blood provides heightened abilities and near immortality. That addictive power, combined with the curse, makes a hunter kill again and again."

I could almost see the wheels turning in her mind. I slid my hand over her hip, drawing her closer.

"That hunter wants your blood?"

"Once maybe. This hunter and I have a history. Now he's out for revenge."

She gasped. "What happened?"

I turned one of his own against him. "We got the upper hand a few months ago and helped another pack capture him, but...he escaped."

Mia lay her head on my shoulder, snuggling in close. "That's why you were so freaked out at the waterfall."

"Not for me. For you." I kissed the top of her head. "Anyone who knows about the shifter world is in danger. I want you to stay with me until it's safe."

She thought for a moment before nodding. "I get it now."

"And stay out of the woods, especially at night."

"I will." She covered a yawn and her eye lids drooped.

"C'mon. Let me take you to bed."

I climbed off the couch and pulled on my jeans, before lifting her and the blanket into my arms. I carried her upstairs and tucked her into bed. She wiggled to one side, and I lay there on top of the covers until she fell asleep. I should check in with my brothers, but I couldn't get my legs to walk back down the stairs.

Instead, I lay there awake for what seemed like hours while Mia slept beside me. Why didn't I feel better? I'd told her what I was and warned her about the hunter, yet, the lead weight in my chest remained. Thanks to the mating bond, my need to be near her was so strong I couldn't think of anything else.

First thing in the morning, I'd tell her. She deserved to know.

A wolf howled in the forest behind Mia's house, interrupting my thoughts. I recognized the call. As quietly as I could, I slipped out of bed and pulled the covers over her shoulders before softly kissing her temple. At the bedroom door, I looked back at her asleep in the bed. My heart swelled. She was here. We were together. For the first time in a long time, maybe things would be okay.

I tiptoed down the stairs, shoved on my shoes and slipped out the back door, jogging to the forest.

Liam stood beside a thick tree trunk with his hands in the pocket of his jeans.

"How'd it go with M—" Liam's nostrils flared with a deep rise of his chest. His eyes widened. "Whoa. You mated with her?"

Was it that obvious?

"Holy fuck. That's one way to tell her. Did she already know?"

"About me being a shifter? Nope, she had no idea. About the mating bond? I haven't raised it yet, but I presume not."

Liam's lips rolled inward forming a grim line. Once again, I wanted to deck him and remind him that he was my younger brother, not the other way around.

"Listen, I don't need any shit about it. I know it wasn't ideal. I didn't exactly plan to complete the mating tonight, it just...happened. I'll tell her everything in the morning."

"What the universe wants, the universe gets."

I craned my neck and stared at the shadowy forest canopy. "I'm beginning to believe that."

I screwed up tonight. Even though Mia said she sensed our connection and agreed we'd waited long enough to be together, I still should've told her the ramifications of two mates having sex.

It sealed the mating bond forever.

"What will you do if she sells the house and leaves?"

Fuck Liam for stating the obvious. I couldn't think about that right now. I'd mated with her, no one else could ever fill the void she'd create if she left. Ever. I'd waited for her and I'd continue to wait for the rest of eternity if it took that.

But would I leave my brothers and my home to follow her?

I glanced back at the house then leveled my brother with a hard stare. "Is there a reason you came here, 'cause I doubt it was just to give me shit."

"A hunter attacked a wolf in Rhett's pack tonight. The pack took him down."

"The same hunter?"

"They think so. I thought you'd wanna know."

Relief burst inside my chest and for the first time in what felt like forever, my lungs inhaled to their full capacity. "Thanks, man."

At least now time was on my side. I didn't need to rush and could tell Mia properly. We could finally start our new life together.

I turned to leave but Liam snagged my shirt.

"You gotta tell her, Noah. This won't end well if you keep it a secret."

I shrugged out of his hold. "I will."

I rolled over, reaching out my arm for Mia but came up empty. My eyes snapped open as I jolted upright. Mia wasn't there. Heart pounding, I bolted out of bed and down the stairs, but skidded to a halt at the back door.

She sat in a chair on the porch, looking like an angel sent from heaven. A vision of light in my dark, dreary existence. With her head angled toward her lap, and white earbuds dangling from her ears, I took my chances sneaking up on her. She didn't even flinch as I slipped out the door and crept up behind her. Leaning over the back of the chair, I nuzzled the spot on her neck where I'd marked her last night.

Her initial squeal lowered to a moan as she tilted her head to one side, giving me better access. I ran with it and trailed kisses along her neck and back up to her jaw. Cupping her cheek, I angled her face toward me and took her mouth, kissing her deep. Before things got too heated and I threw her over my shoulder and stormed inside, I drew back.

I glanced at the sketch pad and cocked a brow. "Should I be jealous of your fascination with my wolf?"

I still couldn't believe she named my wolf after some god.

She laughed and removed the earphones. "Maybe." She wrapped the cord around her cell and lay it on top of the sketch pad, placing them on the floor.

I rounded her chair and leaned forward, bracing my hands on the armrests. "How'd you sleep?"

Her lip kicked up at the corner. "The best I have in years. You?"

"Same." I lowered and brushed my lips over hers. "Thanks to you."

"Well, if you need another good night's sleep, I'm happy to help you out."

"I think that's a brilliant idea." I leaned back slightly. "I spoke to my brother last night. They caught the hunter over in Timber Falls."

She exhaled a slow breath. "I'm glad."

"Me too." I held her gaze for a moment as unsaid words passed between us. Hopes for the future, a silent commitment between two mates. Or maybe it was a one-way conversation from me. "What are your plans for tonight?"

"Why?" A smile gradually grew on her cheeks. "Are you going to take me to another hidden spot?"

"I have something better in mind."

A sexy smirk lifted at the corner of her mouth. "Is that so?"

"Yep, so keep it free. I gotta get a few things done at the bar, but after, you're all mine."

Her smile widened, lighting up her eyes. "I like the sound of that."

"Me too, baby. Me too."

She clutched the front of my shirt and pulled me in, kissing me in a way that made me want to keep the bar closed for a whole week just so we never left her bed. The thought was so damn tempting.

Instead, I drew back and kissed her forehead. "See you tonight."

chapter twelve

Mia

Tiny butterflies fluttered around in my belly each time I thought about seeing Noah. I kept busy by cleaning out Joan's bedroom and the spare closet downstairs, but regardless of my efforts, those butterflies wouldn't settle. I lasted until mid-afternoon before I gave up and headed to the bar and grill.

A drink while I waited for Noah to finish would ease my nerves.

Why was I so nervous? We'd already slept together, technically, we were doing this whole relationship thing in the wrong order anyway.

I pulled up short outside the entrance to Cole's Bar. *Relationship?*

I didn't come to Woodland Falls for a relationship. I came to sell Joan's house so I could finally stand on my own two feet. A relationship was never part of that plan.

What if Noah wanted more?

Of course, he wanted more. He'd waited fifteen years for me to come back here. *I'm his mate.* What did that even mean?

Ugh. I couldn't let all that overwhelm me. Tonight, I just wanted to spend time with Noah, get to know him more, now that I knew his secret.

After composing myself, I strode into the bar. My heart flipped around in its cage the moment I spotted Noah behind the bar, chatting to a woman around the same age. He casually dried a glass, fully engrossed in their conversation. I just hung out at the door staring at him.

A soft smile warmed my cheeks when I thought of the moment he shifted into a wolf. How magical and fascinating the shift was. Then all the things we did last night and how much my feelings for him had grown. For the first time in a long time, someone made me feel not just complete, but worthy.

As though he sensed me standing there, his gaze swung my way. Our eyes locked, and my heart soared. He winked, tipping his chin for me to come closer.

I made my way to the bar and sat on a stool two down from the other woman, shrugged out of my jacket and folded it over the back of the chair.

"Hey there," he said, bracing his hands on the bar top leaning over waiting for a kiss.

I met him halfway and pressed my lips against him. Everything about him, about us, seemed so easy and natural. Were normal couples this comfortable with each other after just one night? Though, I guess, we'd known each other for longer than that. The whole situation was anything but normal.

Noah straightened, that dimple on his cheek deepened sending a little thrill through my middle.

"Hey," I replied.

He motioned to the other woman. "This is Ivy, my brother's wife." He lowered his voice. "Liam's mate."

Oh, secret shifter code.

I turned to Ivy. She was stunning. Deep brown eyes, wavy hair, and a beautiful dusting of pink over her cheeks. "Nice to meet you."

"Welcome to the Cole family, Mia."

My pulse kicked a little. Welcoming me to the family was moving a bit fast, wasn't it?

I made a mental note to ask Noah about what being a mate entailed. Was it like dating? Or more? He'd told me that wolves have one mate for life. If that were true, like I suspected, then I doubted he sought only a girlfriend.

Ivy patted the seat beside her. "Come closer so we can chat." As she spoke, her cell pinged, and she picked it up off the bar to glance at the screen. "Liam's on his way." She placed the phone back down and looked at Noah. "So you can stop babysitting me."

His laugh lit up his unnaturally blue eyes. "You think

this is babysitting? You wanna pray you're not having a girl."

Ivy exhaled a loud exaggerated sigh. "It wouldn't surprise me if you all took shifts sitting on the front porch with shotguns."

Noah laughed again, louder this time. "Don't worry, we've already set up a schedule."

I moved seats and settled in next to Ivy. Her hand rested on a small rounded bump at her belly. "You're pregnant?"

"Yeah." She swiveled to face me. "Can you imagine if it's a girl and the Cole brothers had their way? The poor thing won't be able to date until she's ninety."

Noah rounded the bar to stand behind my chair. He wrapped his arms tight around my middle, resting his chin on my shoulder. "That seems reasonable, right Mia?" His tone left no question about his intention to embrace the overprotective uncle role.

I drew back to see his face. "Hey, don't bring me into this."

"I have a feeling you girls will put the Cole brothers in their place more than once."

"Damn straight," Ivy replied.

I couldn't speak. Having Noah so close, his heat radiating through my back, his cologne consuming my senses.

He angled his head to whisper at my ear. "I have a surprise for you."

I swallowed. "A surprise?"

What could possibly top seeing him shift into a wolf?

"Yep. I was gonna give it to you at dinner, but since you're here..." He kissed my cheek. "Get excited."

Lowering his arms, he returned behind the bar. From under the counter, he grabbed a small cardboard box and held it just out of my reach.

"What is it?" I leaned forward trying to peek.

He snapped it away and grinned. "You have to wait and see."

He turned his back to Ivy and me, and gathered various liquor bottles and items from the fridge. The anticipation killed me. But rather than stare at him, trying to figure it out and ruin the surprise, I swiveled my chair to face Ivy. "How far along are you?"

She smiled, rounding her hand over her belly. "Almost five months, so I still have ages to go."

Something about the way she smiled when she spoke of her pregnancy told me she'd make a great mom. People like her should have babies. People like my mother, not so much. Though, I was thankful she at least had me.

"It'll be fun to have cousins running around crazy at the Cole ranch."

"Does Ashton have kids?"

"No, he hasn't mated yet. I meant when you and Noah have kids."

I swallowed. The fantasy between Noah and I burst in one second. Holy hell, I'd only just met the guy and Ivy thought we'd pop out a few kids. Noah and I hadn't agreed to run away and get married or anything.

Besides, kids were never in my future. I didn't exactly have the best role model. What happened if I turned out like my mother?

Thankfully, before I answered, Noah slid a glass in

front of me. A tall fancy tumbler filled with pale golden liquid and a floating lime wedge.

His smile was contagious.

"Is this a cocktail?"

He leaned in close, his voice low and silky. "If you tell the locals I made you one, you'll ruin my badass reputation."

I laughed so hard I almost fell off my stool.

He nodded to the drink. "Give it a try."

I took a sip through the straw. Fizzy, not overly sweet, and a decent amount of rum. "This is really good. What is it?"

"Dark and Stormy."

How appropriate.

"I thought it was the perfect mix of Woodland Falls meets fancy inner-city cocktail bar." He lifted one shoulder. "Plus, I already had all the ingredients. I only needed to order the glasses."

"Thank you." My heart felt so full that at any minute it would burst from my chest. "I always loved the idea of cocktails, but I never really had the free time to try them."

What I loved even more was that he specially ordered glasses to make the cocktail for me.

I took another sip. Given the lightness sneaking through my shoulders, I think he was a little heavy handed with the rum.

"Hey, bartender." Ivy pointed to my drink. "Does that come in a non-alcoholic version?"

Noah grinned and got to work making Ivy a concoction in the same fancy glass. He slid it to her. As she took her first sip, a man wrapped his arms around her from behind, kissing her cheek.

"I missed you." His hands slid to her belly. "Both of you."

Ivy cupped his cheek with one hand. "You're lucky. This drink is so good I might have gone home with it instead."

The guy growled, nuzzling Ivy's neck. "I bet that drink doesn't satisfy you like I do."

Ivy tapped a finger on her lips, thinking. "This is true. You win. But can we at least stay until I finish it?"

He kissed her forehead. "Take your time. I need to talk to Noah anyway." He straightened, turning to me. "Mia, right? I'm Liam."

I shook his hand. "Nice to meet you."

"Likewise." He glanced to Noah. "You got a second?"

Noah nodded and the two disappeared into a room past the kitchen.

"So," Ivy sipped her drink. "Noah told me you inherited Joan's house."

"I did. But I'd like to have it on the market at the end of summer."

My chest tightened, and I wasn't sure why. I wanted to sell Joan's place. Yet, now saying it aloud stirred this weird feeling. Was it doubt? If so, why? I couldn't rethink my plans just because I'd met an incredible guy who also happened to be the same wolf I befriended as a teenager. The same wolf who'd stolen my heart.

Yet, here I was, reconsidering my plan.

"You're selling it?" Ivy frowned. "Oh. Will another Whitcome buy it?"

"I doubt it. I'm an only child."

Her shoulders relaxed. "That's a relief." She slapped a hand over her mouth. "Oh, my God. I'm sorry. I didn't mean to say that. These damn pregnancy hormones have me jumbling all my words."

She laughed it off, though her tone suggested she knew exactly what she'd said. She sipped her drink.

"Why are you relieved I don't have any siblings?"

Her fingers stilled on the straw, avoiding eye contact. "Ivy."

She slowly turned her head to me, searching my eyes for a moment. "It's really not my place to say."

Prickles raced over my arms. "Say what?"

"Ivy," Liam said, startling me.

I spun to find Liam and Noah standing behind the bar. Color drained from Noah's face.

Liam squeezed his brother's shoulder. "There's no one here. I'll close the door on our way out."

Noah's gaze held mine. He nodded. My heart pounded like crazy. What the hell were they keeping from me?

Ivy slid off the stool. "I'm sorry, Noah."

Liam gathered Ivy's coat and helped her into it. The tension in the bar increased with each second. I jumped when Ivy touched my arm, her face etched with sadness. Without saying another word, she left with Liam.

I waited for the door to close before turning to Noah. "You want to tell me what's going on?"

He rounded the bar to sit on the stool beside me, spinning me and positioning my legs between his. "It doesn't matter. You're nothing like your ancestors."

A weight sank low in my belly. "You know my family?"

Of course, he did. Noah said shifters were near immortal, the Coles had probably lived in Woodland Falls for decades, if not longer. Had my family lived here that long too? My mother grew up here, though from what I knew, she left as a teen after a falling out with Joan.

"Your family knew about us, about the shifter world."

"What?" I whispered the words so softly I hardly heard them. "If that's true, wouldn't I have known?"

Would I? Growing up, I didn't exactly have a great relationship with my mother. She never spoke to me about anything important. She hardly spoke to me at all, too busy organizing where to ditch me before her next work trip. And I'd only spent one summer with Joan.

"Noah." An uneasy feeling prickled along my nape. "What aren't you telling me?"

He met my gaze and in that split second, I wished I hadn't asked. I didn't want to know the answer.

An awful feeling sank low and heavy in my belly.

"The Whitcomes are the original...hunters."

chapter thirteen

Noah

Mia stared at me for so long I wondered if she'd heard me. Did I say it aloud? 'Cause I sure as hell thought about it a million times during the past two weeks. Correction, during the past fifteen years.

Back then I didn't know Mia was a Whitcome. Joan fostered a few kids over the years, and I assumed Mia was one of them.

"What did you say?"

I swallowed. "The Whitcome family are the original hunters. For centuries, they've hunted shifters for their blood, triggering the curse generation after generation."

"No," she whispered. "You're lying."

My heart cracked, splintering into jagged shards. "Why would I lie to you? I have nothing to gain from making this shit up." My stomach twisted. "I have everything to lose."

"Lose?" Her eyes narrowed, then realization dawned on her face. "As in me. Your...mate?"

I nodded.

I let her push my leg aside as she slid off the stool to stand. Secrets had a way of coming out eventually, I knew that, but I wished they weren't mine. I thought I had more time. I wanted to tell her about the mating bond first.

She was nothing like the others of her kind, I sensed that deep in my soul.

Mia paced, stopping in front of a wrought iron wolf head hung on the back wall. She stood there, hands on hips, staring at my family's crest. I hopped off the stool and crossed to her, sliding my hands up and down her arms.

"If Joan was a hunter, why didn't she say anything to me when I came here?"

She twisted to face me, and the look on her face made my knees buckle. Shock, confusion, betrayal. It took every ounce of strength not to sweep her up in my arms and tell her everything would be all right. Would it? I didn't know. Whether we had a future or not depended on this conversation.

I led her to the nearest chair and sat facing her. "Joan was different. She and my dad had an...understanding."

"An understanding not to kill each other?"

"When you put it like that, it sounds a bit bizarre." I took her hand in mine. "Joan had already triggered the hunter curse when my parents moved here but she hated the curse and the compulsion to kill for blood. She and my dad struck a deal. In exchange for his blood to keep the cravings at bay, Joan created a concoction to mask our shifter scent which kept our existence in Woodland Falls a secret, protecting us from other hunters."

She thought for a moment. "My grandmother was an immortal hunter." The creases in her brows deepened. "And my mother? Did you know her? Is she the same?"

I held her gaze. No more secrets. "Yes. But she didn't agree with Joan's deal. From what I know, your mother had a falling out with Joan and left town." I squeezed her hand trying to reassure her. "It doesn't matter what your mother is or isn't like, you're not her. I've known that from the first moment I saw you. I feel it in my soul."

"How can you be sure? I might be. If what you say is true, I have the hunter curse. What if tomorrow or the next day, I wake up and have the urge to kill you for your blood like some sick vampire?"

I held back my smirk. "I have no doubt there'll be times in our lives when you want to kill me. But wanting to and actively trying to are two very different things."

Her brows furrowed. "If my grandma had the blood, how did she die of a heart attack? You said the blood healed and gave her near immortality."

A lump thickened in the back of my throat. Fucking secrets. I should've learned my lesson in the beginning.

"After my parents died, Ash vowed to keep the Cole end of the bargain, but that was right about the time you first came to Woodland Falls." I paused, not sure how to explain it. "I think Joan knew about us. I think she knew you were my fated mate. Right after you left, she told Ash that she'd continue providing us the concoction but no longer wanted blood. She fought against the bloodlust and the compulsion to kill every day."

She sat back in the chair. "That's why your wolf never stepped out of the forest. It always waited at the tree line. Even though you had an agreement, Joan was still your enemy."

I nodded.

"So, she had no blood in her system to prevent the heart attack?"

My pulse kicked up, thumping around my body so fast it made my brain fuzzy. I let go of her hand to wipe mine along my jeans.

"Noah?"

I'd dreaded this moment from the second I found out who she was. No, before that. I'd dreaded this moment ever since Joan died. Ash said not telling Mia and lying weren't the same thing, but it sure felt like they were.

Regardless of what my brothers thought, Mia deserved to know the whole truth. Joan was her grandmother. If she left because of it, then I'd lay my heart at her feet and beg her to stay.

"Noah?"

I lifted my gaze to hers. "Joan didn't die of a heart attack. She died because of me."

There. I said it. I finally fucking said it.

Her eyes gaped open. I tried to grab her hand again, but she pulled it out of my reach. "What?"

I swallowed the big-ass lump blocking my airway. "Someone discovered her secret and that she'd sided with shifters. It wasn't long before a hunter stalked her house, terrorizing her every night but even then, she didn't stop protecting us."

I stared at the ceiling, instead of peering at my shirt half expecting to see a gaping hole where someone had torn out my heart.

"My wolf waited in the forest behind Joan's house every afternoon for years, waiting for you." An imaginary fist squeezed and twisted my heart, but I kept talking. I needed to get it all off my chest. "I became complacent and, I dunno, angry that you never came back. Eventually, I gave up. I figured I'd missed my chance with you and I stopped going to Joan's house. A week later, I sensed something was wrong with her, but I ignored it. That night a fucking hunter attacked her."

Her fingers threaded through mine. "Oh, Noah."

"By the time I swallowed my pride and got there, Joan was dead. Ash and I tracked the hunter all the way to Timber Falls. Before I tore the fucker apart, the local pack threw him in a cell so he could rot as a human and never again have access to shifter blood."

I breathed my first full breath in nearly three months. I urged Mia to stand between my legs and peered up at her. "I'm so sorry."

Her lips rolled inward. "It's not your fault, Noah."

"I stopped going to her house. I stopped protecting her. I failed you."

She slowly shook her head. "No, you didn't. The only one to blame is that hunter." Her eyes widened. "That's why the hunter didn't attack us at the waterfall. He couldn't sense you were a shifter."

I nodded.

"But if the other pack locked him up, how was it the same hunter at the waterfall?"

"Somehow he escaped. But you don't need to worry, the Timber Fall's pack killed him. They're not keen on second chances."

She exhaled a deep breath but remained silent. We'd reached that point where there was nothing more to say. I'd laid it all out for her and now the choice was in her hands. The silence pounded in my ears as I waited.

I couldn't lose her, not again.

"What if I become one of them?"

"You won't. Shifter blood is the only way to trigger the curse. As long as you don't drink the blood, you can fight the compulsion." I pulled her toward me. "I know it's a lot to process."

"You think?" She gaped at me. "In a matter of days, I found out a whole other world exists, and not only am I destined for a guy who can shift into a wolf, but also my family spent years..." Her eyes widened. "Centuries, hunting wolves for their blood."

I held her gaze. "We'll get through this."

She retreated a step, out of my embrace, letting my hands slip from hers. "I need time to figure this out." She took another step backward. Her expression hardened. "I don't even know how to be a mate. I came here to sell Joan's house and set myself up in the city. I didn't come here for..."

Me.

The sentence hung in the air, tearing out my heart. She'd come here with the intention of leaving, she'd made that clear from day one. But I thought I could convince her to stay. Convince her to be with me. Instead, all I'd shown her were death and danger.

I stood. "Let me cook you dinner. I'll answer any questions you have."

She shook her head. "No. I need time to think. Alone."

Without waiting for my reply, she turned and walked out the door. I let her go even though every cell in my body screamed to chase her. She wanted space, I understood that. But I couldn't lose her again. Not after waiting so long for her to come back.

How the hell did I screw this up so badly?

chapter fourteen

Mia

For what seemed like hours, I searched the house looking for something, anything to prove my family were hunters, descendants of witches. The conversation with Noah played on repeat in my mind.

How didn't I know about shifters? Or that I was part of some ancient cursed family, destined to become a hunter? How did that knowledge just skip me? If Joan hadn't died, would she have eventually told me? Did that mean I was also part witch?

"Ugh!" I crawled out of the nook underneath the stairs, banging the back of my head. "Ouch."

I found nothing to suggest that Joan was a sick hunter hellbent on drinking wolf blood for immortality. I gagged at the thought.

But I kept coming back to one question. Why would Noah lie? He had nothing to gain from lying to me. As he said, he had everything to lose.

Which brought me back to the whole mate thing. So many unanswered questions.

In the kitchen, I grabbed a mug to make herbal tea... nope, screw that. I abandoned the tea in favor of bourbon, pouring a generous amount and taking it outside to sit on the back step. The cool night air would do me some good, clear my head and help figure out what to do next.

This late, the forest was eerie. Shadowy branches swayed in the breeze, leaves rustling along the forest floor. Somewhere over to the right, a creature scurried between the trees.

I sipped the bourbon, briefly closing my eyes as the burn traveled down my throat, warming my chest.

The Whitcomes are hunters...

I never saw anything to suggest my mother knew about the shifter world or was a hunter. People who hunted the blood of wolves to become near immortal. My mother wasn't...

"Oh, no."

Every time I saw my mother, which wasn't often, she'd barely aged. Growing up, she constantly dumped me with people so she could go on work trips around the country. Was she...hunting?

Bile rose in my throat.

Had my mother hidden this life from me the entire

time? After the argument she had with Joan when I first came here, Mom never brought me back. Was it because she discovered Joan's secret? Did my mother want me to become a hunter?

Was that why she treated me like such a failure?

I tried to think about everything Joan said to me the summer I spent here. But it was too long ago, I couldn't possibly remember. The only rule Joan had was to stay out of the tool shed. She never warned me about the wolves or hunters. In fact, she often saw me with Noah's wolf. I remember one time, the anguish on her face as she sat on the back porch watching me sketch Thor. I thought she felt sad for hardly seeing her granddaughter. But...

She knew the wolf was a shifter. The wolf knew Joan was a hunter.

The final pieces fell into place.

I lifted the mug to my lips and took a longer sip. It did nothing to calm my fluttering heart, or ease the pain spreading through my chest. My mind wouldn't stop repeating Noah's words. I needed to know for sure. But I'd looked everywhere...

The shed.

Since coming back, I hadn't bothered to look in there, unsure why. Maybe subconsciously I didn't want to know what Joan hid from me. Why was it so important that I not go in there?

I lowered the mug to the floor and stood, peering toward the shed. This late at night, I needed a flashlight. I darted back inside, grabbed one, and returned to the porch, shining the light along the trees until it fell on the tool shed at the far end of the yard.

I hesitated.

The weird sensations swirling in my stomach intensified. I should just take my bourbon and go back inside. Did I really want to know what was in the shed? If I ignored it, I could pretend this world didn't exist and that I wasn't a part of it.

But...that wouldn't work. I needed answers.

Before I wimped out, I jogged down the stairs and across the lawn guided by the flashlight. The door handle of the shed warmed under my touch. Thank goodness it wasn't locked.

Hang on. Why wasn't it locked?

The instant I stepped across the threshold a cold shiver skated down my spine.

Everything's fine, I won't find anything.

I shined the flashlight around the space, landing on the nearest workbench. *What the...?* I crept closer. Jar after jar, filled with leaves, plants, powders. Vines and sticks weaved together in strange hanging ornaments like on those supernatural TV shows I watched. More proof Joan was a witch.

Tucking the flashlight under my arm, I screwed the lid off one jar and lifted it to my nose. Dried herbs.

That wasn't so bad.

I swept the light around the space, turning in a full circle. At the far end, an oversized metal cabinet caught my attention, and I gravitated to it. My hands shook so much I barely unlatched the lock.

Dread rolled around in my belly.

I creaked open the door and aimed the flashlight on the contents.

I gagged, slapping a hand over my mouth.

More jars stacked the shelves. Only this time, not filled with dried herbs, but...bits. Fingers, eyeballs, fur, pieces of flesh floating in pale orange liquid. I gagged again, inspecting the closest jar. Inside were two amber eyeballs.

Did Joan use them in the concoction she gave the Cole family? Or had she used them to fight the hunter compulsion?

A wolf howled deep in the forest, startling me. I cocked my ear in the direction. The howl sounded different, not Noah. Maybe one of his brothers?

I waited. Listened. When the wolf didn't howl again, I turned away from the cabinet and aimed the flashlight at the roof. The metal cabinet was nothing compared to this. Huge animal traps hung from the solid timber beams, chunky meat cleavers, rusted metal chains. The shed resembled a freaking horror movie.

Sick to the stomach, I spun to leave. The flashlight landed on a thick, leather bound book with an ancient symbol embossed on the cover. *Oh, no.* I inched closer. I opened the book and flicked through the pages. Spells. Hundreds of them. Pictures of the same woven sticks and vines that hung in the shed, sketches of wolves, and strange symbols.

This wasn't an ordinary old book. This was a grimoire.

A folded piece of parchment tucked between the pages caught my attention. I slipped it out and aimed the flashlight so I could read it. It contained a detailed Whitcome family tree at the top of the page, ending with my name. Below was a list of about a dozen surnames with one underlined, written above all the others.

Elizabeth Whitcome.

I staggered back.

Noah was right. The Whitcomes were hunters. But not just any hunters. I had an awful feeling my ancestor was the powerful witch who created the curse.

Chills scratched along my spine.

A wolf howled again. This time the lead weight sank lower in my stomach. Something was wrong. I dug my hand in my back pocket reaching for my cell only to realize I'd left it on the porch.

Damn it.

Noah said they caught the hunter from the waterfall, that the forest was safe. But was it? Oh, dear Lord, with Joan dead, would more hunters come here to search for shifters? Were they related to me?

As a teenager, I always felt safe in the woods. Clearly, that safety was thanks to Joan and all this magical witch business. Plus, I hadn't lied when I said Thor protected me. He was with me every time I ventured into the forest and never left my side.

I should call Noah. I didn't like what he said, but he'd told me the truth. I had so many questions and only he could answer them.

I closed the cupboard and turned to leave.

From the corner of my eye, a shadow passed the window of the shed. I stilled. Was it Noah? One of his brothers?

Someone else?

I switched off the flashlight until I knew for sure. In

the darkness, my pulse whooshed in my ears. My heart lodged in my throat as the seconds ticked by, ears straining with every slight sound.

Gravel crunched around the side of the shed, moving toward the door. It creaked open. A shadowy figure loomed in the doorway.

I dropped to the floor, huddling behind a bench.

"I know you're in here." A deep menacing voice made the hairs at the back of my neck stiffen. "I can smell you."

Noah

My cell rang again, and Ash's picture flashed on the home screen. I tossed it on the passenger seat and let it go to voicemail. For the fourth time.

I loved my brothers, but sometimes they just needed to back off and give me space.

After Mia left the bar, I locked up and drove. Without a destination in mind, I kept the foot on the gas, heading aimlessly down the highway.

Foreboding swirled in my gut all afternoon, and it wouldn't let up. I put it down to offloading all those secrets to Mia, and given we'd had sex, it awoke the ancient bond between us. I sensed her uncertainty, her unease. All her emotions collided inside me confusing the hell out of me.

My cell rang again, this time Liam.

"For fuck's sake."

Knowing they wouldn't give up until I checked in, I pulled the truck to the side of the road and answered.

"What?" I barked.

"Where the fuck are you?" Liam snapped.

At his tone, adrenaline surged through my veins, muscles coiled tight, preparing for action. My wolf, who'd paced back and forth all afternoon, now clawed against my insides growling to shift.

Before I even registered my movements, I turned the truck around and sped back to Woodland Falls.

"Twenty miles out of town. Why?"

"Is Mia with you?"

All that adrenaline coiled into a knot. I accelerated. "No. What the hell's going on?"

"Baker called. He caught one of their shifters working with a hunter."

I waited for the punch line. Shifters working with hunters wasn't the most shocking news of the decade. Hell, even we did...before Joan died.

"Spit it out, Liam."

"The one they caught yesterday wasn't the hunter who killed Joan. The sick sonofabitch is still out there."

"Fuck."

"That's not all. Baker tortured the shifter. He said since escaping, the hunter has been hiding in Woodland Falls."

The truck's engine whined as my foot slammed against the floor. Violent tremors quaked my body, my wolf getting impatient. Liam needed to talk faster. I could only hold off the shift for so long. Shifting while I drove wasn't the smartest idea.

"I'll call Mia."

"Ash already tried. He assumed you were together but when she didn't answer and neither did you, he shifted and headed to her place."

Thank fuck. I just hoped she was there, locked inside the house.

"I'll meet Ash there."

"Baker is on the way with a few others from Rhett's pack."

At least we had backup coming. We needed all the help we could get to take down this psycho once and for all.

I just hoped I got there in time.

chapter fifteen

Mia

"You mated with one," the guy sneered. His tone filled with so much disgust and hatred it made my knees shake.

I bit down hard on my bottom lip to prevent from making a sound.

Mated? More questions flooded my mind. All I knew for sure was that I needed to remain hidden. If I didn't, I had no doubt this guy would kill me.

As quietly as I could, I snuck backward, bracing myself on the bottom shelf of a workbench. My fingers landed on something long and sharp. A knife?

"You're a traitor," he roared, slamming something hard against the outside of the shed. "Just like your grandmother."

I bit my lip again to prevent crying out.

This creep wasn't just someone who knew Joan. He was a hunter. Most likely the one who killed her for betraying their disgusting so-called legacy.

A wolf howled again, the same one as before, closer this time. Another joined the call, coming from the opposite direction.

Noah's brothers? Were they coming here?

I hoped not. If the wolves came, the hunter would slaughter them. He'd kill all of us. Everything Joan did to protect me, to protect the Cole family, would be for nothing.

I frantically tried to figure a way out of this. A way for all of us to make it out alive.

My stomach rolled, swishing around until I thought I'd vomit. I couldn't just hide in the shed all night and do nothing. I needed to help.

I curled my fingers around the knife. A strange wave of adrenaline coursed through my blood while I familiarized myself with its length and weight. Longer and thicker than a kitchen knife but more jagged with a heavier handle. A knife wasn't as effective as a shotgun, but let's face it, I had no experience fighting with either.

Distracting the hunter bought the wolves valuable time.

With the knife gripped tight in my hand, I straightened my legs slowly and quietly, peeling myself off the ground. Hunching over at the waist so the hunter didn't spot me, I snuck around the workbench and halted by the door.

The rolling in my stomach solidified, forming a massive lead weight. Even with my heart lodged firmly at the base of my throat, the hand clutching the knife remained calm and steady. Was it because of the hunter curse? Was part of me subconsciously prepared and conditioned to fight even though I'd only just discovered my heritage?

I hoped so.

I inhaled several slow, deep breaths until my heartrate leveled. The wolves silenced. I guessed they were closer now, stalking through the forest, preparing to strike. I just needed to keep the hunter distracted.

I could do this.

I peeked my head around the workbench to spot where the hunter—

All at once, the hunter lunged at me. Deep orange light erupted inside the shed. A translucent shield flared in the doorway. I screamed, falling on my ass, scurrying backward. The knife skidded across the floor.

Some badass fighter I was.

The hunter shrieked, his arm caught between layers of pulsing light in the doorway. The sickening smell of burning flesh made me gag.

The hunter jerked his arm free from the magical shield.

"You bitch," he roared with so much menace it made my bones rattle. "I'll gut you along with your wolf."

Then, as if he'd never been there, the hunter spun and dashed around the side of the shed.

What. The. Hell?

How did a magical shield prevent the hunter from entering the shed, but not me?

A wolf snarled. I climbed onto the workbench to peer out the window, but I couldn't see a damn thing. How long would the shield last? Would it hurt me? How did it work?

Gah! I didn't have time to figure any of that out. I needed to help before the hunter killed the wolf.

Taunting words echoed through the night coming from the hunter, answered by the snarling wolf. With the hunter distracted, I could sneak out.

I slid off the bench and using the light from the shield, found my knife on the ground beside the workbench. With it once again in my hand, I crept toward the doorway. The light vanished, no longer a magic flesh-burning barrier, returning the shed to complete darkness.

I inhaled a deep breath, then slid my foot along the floor to the threshold...waited...and slid it past. Nothing happened. Slowly, I reached my arm through the doorway. It didn't burn me.

Joan must've put a spell on the shed so only she and I could enter.

With the knife held low and tight, I crept out of the shed, breathing a sigh of relief when it didn't explode with light. At the edge, I pressed my body flat against the wall and peeked around the corner. At the far end of the yard, just near the forest, a wolf circled the hunter. From this distance and in the dark, I couldn't tell if the wolf was Noah. But I sensed it wasn't.

My gaze darted to the house. I had a clear path to the

back door. If I bolted, I could make it inside before the hunter caught me. I could call for help. Who? The sheriff? Did the sheriff know? Was he a shifter or a witch or a hunter? I had no clue.

Going inside meant abandoning the wolf to fight this battle alone. Joan protected the Coles by never revealing their secret. If I let one of them die because I wasn't brave enough to help, I'd never forgive myself.

I glanced back at the wolf and hunter snarling at each other. The wolf lunged, but the hunter was quicker, darting sideways. Midair, the hunter swiped his arm, striking the wolf with a blade. The wolf yelped but landed on all fours, circling the hunter as though the wound barely registered.

I couldn't just stand there. Fighting the hunter wasn't just the wolf's battle, it was mine. This was my legacy.

I glanced at the trees nearest to the shed. I could use the forest to sneak up behind the hunter. Just as I turned to run, a second wolf sped around the side of the house gunning for me. My heart stilled.

Thor.

He ran so fast I had no time to react. Once at my feet, he growled, pushing me back toward the shed.

"No." I shooed him.

He didn't listen. Thor snapped at my ankles, forcing me backward. I understood his need to protect me, but I wouldn't let him shove me aside.

Near the shed door, out of sight, I crouched, eye level with Thor. "I want to help."

The hunter must've got the upper hand because the other wolf yelped again. Thor snapped his head in that direction at the same time I did. I snuck past him to look around the corner. The other wolf lay on its side, howling in pain. The hunter closed in, raising his blade in the air preparing to strike. Thor looked between me and his fallen brother.

"Go." I shoved him away. "Save him."

Thor held my gaze. I held my breath, waiting, as though the future depended on this decision. In a heartbeat, he turned and ran, launching at the hunter's back. But before he connected, the hunter twisted with unnatural speed, his blade narrowly missing Thor.

Realization struck me hard like a punch in the gut. The hunter almost stabbed not just Thor...but Noah.

They engaged in a vicious brawl. I couldn't watch. Instead, I stared at the injured wolf. He still hadn't moved off the ground. Without thinking, I ran, trying damn hard not to look at Noah in wolf form fighting the hunter. I kept my gaze on the fallen wolf.

When I reached the wolf, I fell to my knees beside him.

Several different howls echoed through the woods. Help was on the way. I needed to keep this wolf alive until they got there.

Blood poured from somewhere on the wolf's belly where the hunter struck him. I could hardly see. Growling and snarling continued behind me as Noah battled the hunter.

With my hand, I search for the wound, smoothing my fingers along the wolf's underbelly. There. Thick warm blood spilled over my fingers.

Something white flashed out of the corner of my eye.

In a split second, everything changed. A white wolf charged toward me. I grabbed my knife, half twisted—

The wolf slammed into my back, smashing me against the ground with the knife beneath me. Hot pain sliced through my stomach. My vision blurred. I grunted, twisting to move. The wolf's jaws snapped at my ear, its foul breath, and the sick smell of blood in its mouth made me gag. I tried to move again but the wolf snarled, pinning me to the ground. I clawed the dirt trying to escape.

Instead of screaming, a choked cry escaped my lips. In the commotion, I couldn't tell if the wolf wanted to kill me or protect me.

Without warning, another wolf attacked it, shoving the first one off my back, releasing the weight. The two wolves tumbled away in a vicious fury of bites and growls. My lungs inhaled but the breath caught midway. Fire burned through my body, the muscles in my stomach spasmed. I coughed, drawing my legs in, curling into a ball, attempting to ease the intense pressure. Nothing helped.

Using all my strength, I rolled onto my back. I instinctively reached for the source of the pain and curled my fingers around the knife lodged deep in my stomach.

Someone screamed Noah's name. My ears buzzed. I coughed, more like gurgled, as blood bubbled up my throat.

When faced with death, people said their life flashed before their eyes. That didn't happen for me. Instead, I saw glimpses of Noah, of what we could've been. Of the life I could've had if I stayed with Joan.

I drifted off in the fantasies. The pain didn't hurt so much anymore. Someone lifted my head off the ground.

"Mia."

Noah. His voice sounded all wrong, strangled, a distant echo over crashing waves.

I rolled my head toward the sound. A heavy weight pressed against my lungs making it impossible to breathe let alone move. I wanted to cough again, clear my throat, but lacked the energy to do either.

Something caressed my cheek, but I barely registered the touch.

"Baby, open your eyes."

Had I closed them? They were too heavy to open. Instead, I smiled. Noah was okay, that was all that mattered. Me on the other hand...

***

Noah

Blood. So much fucking blood. Not just on my hands, but everywhere I looked. Fueled on nothing but revenge and a dangerous amount of hatred, I tore that hunter to bits and regretted nothing. I didn't give a shit about any of it. Spilled blood was the price in war, and we deserved victory. For Joan, and everything she represented.

Now, back in human form, the only blood I cared about was the thick liquid creating a dark stain around the knife lodged in Mia's stomach. A knife she had so bravely gripped in her hand.

I curled my fingers around the handle about to pull it out.

"Don't." Ash snapped, stilling my hand.

Something fractured inside my chest. "I gotta save her."

"If you remove the knife, she'll bleed out."

I didn't even know how it happened. I remembered shifting in her front yard, Ash in wolf form, injured, the hunter about to kill him. I had flashes of Baker's wolf on top of Mia threatening to tear out her throat. Her chocked scream as she fought to free herself.

Soon-to-be-dead Baker approached from my side, his steps slow, hesitant. "I didn't know it was her, Noah. Shit. I'm so sorry. I thought she was with the hunter."

I didn't even spare Baker a glance. As it was, red dotted my vision and it took every ounce of strength not to tear him apart like I had the hunter. I'd deal with him after.

Instead, I poured all my concentration into Mia.

I caressed her pale cheek. "C'mon baby, open your eyes."

Ash crouched beside me, the gash in his side almost completely healed. He inspected the dark red stain expanding around the knife lodged in Mia's stomach. "Baker, is your healer with you?"

Baker must've shaken his head because a second later, Ash cursed.

"Go inside the house, grab towels, blankets, anything you can get your hands on to slow the bleeding."

Baker didn't question the instructions, even though Ash wasn't his Alpha. He bolted toward the house.

Ash moved to lift Mia's shirt and something inside me snapped. I clenched his wrist, stopping him. An unearthly growl rumbled through the night, coming from my chest.

He met my gaze for a second before shaking his head. "There's only one way to save her, Noah. She won't recover from this on her own."

Deep down, I knew that. I just couldn't bring myself to do it. "I won't. Not without her consent."

"Noah, listen to me. You'll never get her to a hospital in time." He leveled his stare with mine. "She'll die. Do you get that? Your mate will die."

I lifted Mia, cradling her head in the crook of my arm. How had everything gone so fucking wrong? Ever since that hunter came to Woodland Falls, he'd torn apart my life.

But Joan's death brought Mia back to Woodland Falls. A second chance I never thought I'd get. I'd waited fifteen years to start a lifetime with my mate. If I didn't save her now, that fucking hunter won.

I stared down at Mia in my arms. Her face sickly pale, her breathing labored. She made wheezy coughing noises as blood filled her lungs.

I was out of time. If I didn't save her now, it would be too late.

After, if she hated me, even if she sold the house and moved back to the city wanting never to see me again, at least she'd be alive. I'd already resigned myself to becoming the lone wolf I feared. If it meant saving her, I'd welcome centuries of loneliness with open arms.

What I couldn't do was exist knowing I could've saved her and chose not to.

I leaned down close to her ear. "I'm sorry, Mia. I can't let you die. I won't." I thrust my free arm to Ash. "Do it."

Without another word, Ash grabbed the hunter's blade off the ground and used it to slice my wrist. Blood dripped down my arm. Shifter blood, the only thing that would save Mia.

I eased my wrist against her lips. "Drink, baby. Heal."

She didn't react. She lay there motionless.

I wouldn't let another person die because of me. I came into her life, I showed her the shifter world, I claimed her as my mate. Everything that happened over the past few weeks was because of me.

"Mia. Drink."

I wiggled my wrist between her lips.

Ever so lightly, her tongue lapped at the cut. Tentative at first, then with more strength, more urgency. Through our bond, I sensed my lifeblood seeping into her mouth, down her throat, repairing damaged organs, sealing torn tissue, breathing life into her lungs.

Her hands shot up and gripped my wrist, holding it in place. Her lips formed a hard seal around the cut, drawing deep pulls of blood. And her moans sent a flash of heat right to my cock. Clearly, she hadn't drained all my blood.

Now that she was out of the danger zone, I sensed the other shifters back off and give us privacy. Thank fuck. 'Cause healing my mate was the most erotic thing I'd ever experienced and I sure as hell didn't need an audience.

Too soon, Mia's lips relaxed, and she eased back from my wrist. Her eyes opened and her gaze locked on mine. Clear, bright eyes full of life, flashed with amber.

In that moment, she became the enemy.

chapter sixteen

Mia

At some point, I passed out. Or drifted off to some faraway land, I couldn't be sure. Too many weird sensations flowed through my veins that I had trouble distinguishing between them. Someone carried me inside and upstairs to my room. Most likely Noah. On and off, I woke and found him curled in an armchair in the corner of the room. Blood still smattered his face, a blanket covered his legs.

This time when I woke, my vision was clearer, brighter, more focused. Strength like I'd never felt before flowed through my limbs. Man, I could run a marathon right now.

Hesitantly, I rolled onto my side facing the window. The same window where I'd first seen Noah's wolf. Funny how things happened in a full circle.

Movement in the corner of the room caught my attention. Noah straightened in the chair. His gaze locked with mine and all those strange sensations once again rushed through my blood. As though someone had injected a magnet into my veins, and it snapped me toward Noah. My heart beat, yet, it felt like another beat alongside it.

But amongst all the confusion, one blissful sensation bloomed between my legs, aching with more intensity than ever before.

Clearly, I was on some awesome pain meds.

Noah peeled himself off the chair and approached the bed, sitting down beside me. His tender touch stroked up and down my cheek, flaming the tingles through my middle.

"How do you feel?"

Hmm. I wasn't sure how to answer that. I felt alive. Freaking turned on. Yet, something had changed, something I couldn't explain.

I pushed myself into a sitting position, scooting back to lean against the headboard. I still wore the same clothes I had on when the hunter attacked. The memories flashed in my mind so fast it caused a dull ache in my temples. I squeezed them, closing my eyes for a second until it passed.

I peered at the slice in my shirt just under my ribs

where a knife had lodged in my stomach. I lifted the fabric, expecting to see a scar or stitches. Nothing. All that remained was a faint, jagged line.

I lowered my shirt and glanced at Noah. "I feel okay, I guess. How did I...survive that?" Blood still lingered on my tongue and down my throat. I exhaled a ragged breath. "I thought I was going to die."

He took my hand in his and stared at it for a long moment. When he lifted his gaze to mine, his eyes were darker, bordering on...sad.

"You were..." Muscles popped along his jaw. "I saved you."

A knot tightened in my gut making me almost afraid to ask. "How?"

"I gave you my blood."

I jerked my hand from his. "What the hell? You told me that triggered the hunter curse." I gasped. "I'm a..."

"I did what I had to. I won't let you die, Mia."

My stomach churned. Was that what all those sensations were? The curse?

Sure, it saved my life, but I didn't consent to any of this. He knew how much I didn't want this. I'd told him. Hadn't I?

Pressure squeezed my lungs. I couldn't breathe. "I'm going to turn into a blood-thirsty psycho."

"No, baby."

He reached for my hand, but I recoiled. Those muscles popped again in his jaw.

"You're not the same as them. Joan refused to kill, you can also. You'll still live for as long as me because we're mated. You don't need the blood and if you crave it, I'll give it to you."

His eyes widened for a split second as though he realized what he'd just said.

"What do you mean we're mated?"

The hunter said the same thing.

His chest rose in fell in a deep inhale. "Remember when I told you that you're my mate?"

I nodded, my throat way too dry to even contemplate replying.

"When we had sex, we sealed the bond between us." He paused for a moment as though searching for words. "It's like a scent, a feeling, an invisible thread that joins two mates."

He reached for my hand again and this time I let him, too overwhelmed to pull away.

To be honest, mating didn't sound that bad. So why the hell did he look like he'd delivered me a life sentence? I didn't want to rush him, but I swear my patience wore thin and I was so over surprises. "What aren't you telling me?"

His eyes darkened. "It's for life. Nothing can break it. Once a shifter mates, they can never complete the bond with another. For humans, it's like marriage I guess, but forever."

"Marriage?" My voice rose. "And you didn't think to mention this when we had sex? Or before?"

"Everything happened so fast, I showed you my wolf, and...we got caught up in the moment."

I hugged my knees to my chest. I didn't want to sound ungrateful, but holy shit. He mated with me. Sure, he saved my life, but...*Gah.* I couldn't even think properly.

"You committed me to something I knew nothing about? Will I change into a wolf now?"

He held back a smirk which only annoyed me further. Did he think this was a joke? Once again, someone else made decisions regarding my life and left me to pick up the pieces.

"No. You'll always be human. You'll just age slower, at the same rate as me."

"Wrong." I glared at him. "I'll always be a hunter."

He flinched. Good. He should feel horrible for what he did. Noah took away my choice, just like everyone else in my life up to this point. My mother, every time she dumped me at someone's house or left me alone to fend for myself. Joan, when she forced me to stay at her house before I inherited it. And now him, signing me up for a life-long commitment without my consent.

This conversation was too much. I couldn't deal with any of it right now.

"You took away my choice, Noah. Twice."

He looked as though I'd just shoved my hand in his chest and ripped out his heart, to tear it to pieces in front of him. Or maybe that was my heart.

"I'm sorry. I'll apologize every second of every day if that's what it takes to earn your forgiveness." His expression hardened, deepening the grooves in his forehead. "But I won't apologize for saving your life. Ever."

It all came down to that one point. Regardless of the mating bond thingy, he'd saved my life. But in doing so, he'd triggered the sick hunter curse lingering inside me.

Part of me screamed to forgive him. How could he possibly ask my consent while I lay there dying? But I just couldn't. I'd had enough of people making choices for me. I came here so I could finally set myself up and he charged in and ruined everything.

"I failed Joan. After all she did to protect my family, I wasn't there to protect her, and she paid for it with her life. I won't let that ever happen to you."

Was he freaking kidding? "So, that's all this is? Some messed up quest for redemption?"

He flinched again and I sensed I hit a nerve, which made me furious. Did he heal me to clear his conscience?

He tilted his head, studying me. His gaze narrowed. "Don't do this. I know what you're thinking and it's not true."

"Really? Because I think you saved me just so you didn't repeat your mistake with Joan."

Those muscles in his jaw popped like crazy. "You're my mate, Mia. I saved you because the thought of spending forever without you fucking kills me."

Maybe that was true. But from the beginning, he'd kept things from me. He kept the fact he was a wolf, that my family were psychos who hunted his blood. He even kept the mating bond from me but was perfectly okay having sex and not telling me about the consequences.

I no longer knew what to believe or who to trust.

I yanked the blanket up to my chin, clutching the ends in my hands as though it would protect my heart from inevitable heartbreak. I was so sick of people dictating how I lived my life, what I did, and the choices I made. Enough was enough. Now was the time I took back control and lived the life I wanted.

"You should leave." My voice choked on the words, even though this was the only way forward.

Noah's lips formed a thin, grim line. He stood, shoving his hands in his jean pockets. "I'll wait downstairs."

My heart splintered with what I needed to say. "No, Noah. I want you to leave. I need to figure this out. Who I am, what all this means. I've barely had time to breathe and suddenly I mated a wolf and triggered a curse that at any moment, will make me want to kill you. God, I have a mother out there somewhere who hid this from me my entire life and she could be hunting shifters as we speak." My vision blurred. "It's too much."

"Don't do this, Mia. I'll prove to you that you won't kill me for my blood. I know you're different. You're not like your mother."

There it was. He'd nailed my greatest fear.

Until I met Noah, my heart had never felt so full, so complete, like I belonged. But I couldn't allow this to continue. He turned out to be like everyone else in my life.

I straightened my shoulders, summoning my last shred of courage and strength. "Everyone I've ever loved has betrayed me with secrets and lies. I don't need more of that, not now, not ever." I met his gaze and didn't waver, not even when tears burned behind my eyes. "I don't want this life."

chapter seventeen

Mia

Warmth tingled across the back of my neck as something stirred behind my heart telling me Noah was here. Again.

For four days, I'd avoided him by focusing all my attention on cleaning Joan's house. But he kept coming back.

I padded up the stairs to the window. The same window where I first saw Noah in wolf form, waiting in the forest for me. Pulling back the drapes, I peered at the spot. Thor stood there, waiting for me.

My heart cracked and I doubt it would ever repair

itself. Every time I spared a glance out the window to the backyard, Noah or Thor stood in the same location. He'd left my house like I'd asked, but he hadn't left me. He hadn't given up.

Had I?

I didn't know. Mating with me without my knowledge, I could probably forgive. We were both caught up in the moment and I was as much to blame as him. When I thought back to that night, he'd tried to tell me something, tried to slow things down, but I hadn't wanted any of that. I'd only wanted him.

Now that bond connected us for life.

To say I didn't feel any different was a lie. When I stopped and thought about it, an invisible thread drew me to Noah before we sealed our bond. Destiny pulled us together the moment I stepped into his bar.

No, even before that. His wolf. Fifteen years ago, that same invisible thread lured me to a wolf lurking in the forest behind this house. I mean, since when did a wolf and a teenage girl ever become best friends?

Thor's head turned my way and his gaze held mine.

I mentally searched inside me for...something. Hatred, the desire to kill, a thirst for his blood. Anything to remind me that Noah had triggered the hunter curse. Did it awake instantly, or did it happen over time? Not knowing the answers to any of this frustrated the hell out of me. If I stayed, if I allowed myself to build a future with Noah, would I wake up one day wanting to drain his blood?

Until I was positive I wouldn't, I couldn't be with him. I couldn't risk it.

No matter how much I loved him—*Oh, God.* The fluttering in my stomach when I thought of him, the deep yearning inside my chest to forgive him. Those feelings weren't the result of our mating bond. I loved him. Despite his actions, despite our different worlds, and the curse that threatened to tear us apart, I damn well loved him.

How did I not see that?

I longed for a home and a family who loved me back, and with Noah, I could have all that. But I was a freaking hunter. A danger to them all. Staying in Woodland Falls put not just Noah in danger, but every other shifter. The Cole family. Ivy and Liam's baby.

I focused on Thor. His front paws inched onto the grass. That dull ache in my heart intensified, consuming my lungs and every other half-dead organ in my chest.

My whole life I'd bounced from one situation to the next, living in the shadows of everyone else's choices and expectations. I'd come to Woodland Falls aching to stand on my own two feet. To create my own path, not one forged on the choices of others.

Today, I took back control.

If Noah wouldn't let me go, then I needed to make that choice for the both of us. I needed to leave. I refused to tear apart their family because of some ancient curse thrust upon mine. A family I no longer held ties with.

I couldn't risk staying here any longer.

With one final glance at Thor, at Noah, I released the drapes and held my breath until they fell back into place. I turned from the window. Noah wanted me to meet him halfway, but this time I wouldn't.

This moment wasn't the start of our epic love story. This was the moment I ended the Whitcome hunters forever.

***

Noah

I sensed Ash approach from behind, but I didn't bother turning to greet him.

"Has she come out yet?" he asked when he stood beside me.

I shook my head. She hadn't peered out the window for forty-eight hours.

For six days, I'd parked my ass in the woods behind her house, alternating between wolf and human form. We both ached for her, so it was only fair that we took shifts. Each afternoon, I caught her peering down from her bedroom window as she had fifteen years ago, but unlike then, she never met me halfway.

Even though I hated myself for doing this to her, to us, I didn't regret it. Not for one second. I would tear myself apart, a slow and miserable death, if it meant saving her life.

Ash squeezed my shoulder. "I thought she'd come out and tell you."

I knew that tone and it wasn't good. "Tell me what?"

"She came to see me today."

My heart stilled. Seeing Ash was progress. Eventually, she'd see me, and I could apologize again. I wasn't kidding when I said I'd apologize every day for the rest of eternity.

But the look on Ash's face, combined with the sudden churn in my gut, told me otherwise. "Is she okay?"

He didn't answer.

"Spit it out, Ash." I growled, growing more impatient by the second.

Ash glanced between the house and me. "She's leaving. Tomorrow. She came to see me about the will."

My heart bled out right there in the woods. "What did you say? I thought she had to stay until the end of the summer."

I thought I had more time.

"Technically, she can leave. She's not putting the house up for sale until the end of the summer and she did live in it while she was here." Ash shoved his hands in his pockets. "I think given the circumstances..."

My fucking brother betrayed me. My own flesh and blood.

"You asshole." Fist clenched, I spun and swung at Ash's face.

He caught my fist in his hand, then shoved it away. "You need to get your head out of your ass and wake up."

"How can I? I drew her into this. Before she came here, she didn't even know about shifters, about me, about her family. If I hadn't told her, she would've gone on oblivious to everything."

"I don't believe that, and I doubt you do either. Joan left her the house for a reason. She wanted her to come back here. Why else include the condition in her will?"

"I've done nothing but break her trust. I wanted to atone for failing Joan, but more than that, I wanted my mate. I fell in love with her before I knew what the word even meant. Now I've ruined everything."

"Instead of moping around in the forest hoping she'll come to you, go fight for her."

"She'll never forgive me, no matter what I do."

"Do I need to punch you? Of course, she won't forgive you while you're hiding out here like a stray pup."

Ash glanced toward the sky, then back at me.

"You told me she was your mate. You've known that for fifteen years."

I scoffed. "That's rich coming from someone who doesn't believe in mates."

"I never said I didn't believe. I just don't believe there's one for me. But I've witnessed the connection—with Mom and Dad, Ivy and Liam. I know it exists. And from what I've seen, nothing breaks a mating bond. Not even an ancient curse."

He paused and my rage simmered.

"I think Joan knew that as well. After she stopped taking the blood, why do you think she still made that god-awful concoction to protect us? Because it also protected you. We all saw how she drove herself crazy trying to break the curse and I think when she realized you and Mia were fated, she finally discovered a way. Think about it. A hunter mated to a shifter. Joan made sure the Whitcome curse ended with the two of you."

I kicked the dirt with my boot and thought for a moment. Joan did stop taking blood, but I assumed she did it because Dad died. Which happened around the time Mia came to stay with her. Did she sense the connection? Did she really believe Mia and I mating would break the hunter curse?

Ash squeezed my shoulder.

"You know what you need to do. Go do it."

I stared at the house as the lights came on in the upstairs bedroom. I held my breath, waiting. A heartbeat later, the drapes pulled back and Mia peered out the window. Our eyes locked and, in that moment, I knew Ash was right.

What was with my brothers always being right?

I needed to fight for Mia. Regardless of everything that happened between us, and our two opposing worlds, and what our future held, she was my mate.

I'd die before losing her again.

chapter eighteen

Mia

I grabbed my jacket and took one final glance around the living room. I'd packed most of Joan's things into three separate boxes: donate, trash, and keep. That last box came with me in the car because I'd never return. It contained keepsakes like photo albums I'd found under the stairs, some of Joan's jewelry, other odds and ends, plus the wolf sketch. I also kept Joan's grimoire because one day, I dunno, maybe I'd want to explore my heritage. Maybe I'd try to be more like Joan. If I could fit the whole house in my apartment back in the city, I'd probably take it all.

I guess I tried to hold on to the past, to the small connection that gave me a family. Holding on to a life I'd never have.

More than a thousand times, I'd questioned if I'd made the right decision. I originally came here to sell Joan's estate and start over, but so much had happened since. I'd reconnected with my wolf, met and fell in love with a shifter, and became a hunter. I didn't know which part shocked me the most. The fact that I'd given my heart away when I never thought I would, or that I belonged to an ancient magical world.

And amongst all that, I'd freaking married a guy by having sex.

Deep inside, I suspected we were kindred spirits or lovers in a past life, from the beginning. Was it so farfetched to believe that by having sex, we sealed the bond between us? *No.* And that bothered me the most. The fact I believed it when Noah said our night together sealed our bond. I couldn't deny it. I felt it.

Then along came the whole ancient curse thing.

Gah!

The house was clean, tidy, and presentable. I'd decluttered the rooms as best I could, donating some furniture to the local charity. At one stage, I considered burning down the shed of horrors, but chickened out. I didn't want to trigger any more curses.

Would the house sell for a reasonable price? I had no idea. All that mattered was the agent suspected it'd sell quickly.

I just wasn't sure how I felt about it anymore. That pang inside my chest wouldn't go away.

No more doubting.

With a heavy heart, I composed myself before walking out of the house for the final time, closing the door behind me.

I drew up short.

Noah sat lengthways along the top step with his legs crossed at the ankles.

He stood and I backed against the front door.

In a heartbeat, he closed the distance between us and took my mouth with his. The kiss punched me right in my heart, breathing life back into it. Full of not just longing and desire, but hope, love, and something I'd begun to associate with our mate bond. As his tongue teased mine, my heart burst into a million petals floating up to the clouds.

I wish he'd stayed away. Saying goodbye only made it harder to leave.

He drew back, leaving me gasping for breath, cradling my face between his strong hands.

I stared into those mesmerizing ice-blue eyes. "You shouldn't be here."

"I'm coming with you," he whispered, a smile hinting on his cheeks.

My heart skipped, but I shut it down.

I closed my eyes briefly. "What if I don't want you to?"

"Too bad." His thumbs stroked along my cheeks, stirring all those sensations in my belly. "There's no way in hell I'm going to sit here and wait another fifteen years for you to come home. We're in this together."

I wasn't so easily convinced. "I...we, have a lot to sort

out. Including the fact I might wake up one day and want to kill you. What then?"

"For as long as we knew Joan, she never stopped trying to break the curse. Ash and I think by us mating, we finally did. Think about it. When the hunter stabbed Ash and he was on the ground, you didn't drink his blood or try to kill him. You tried to save him." He smoothed the back of his hand along my cheek. "Do you have the urge to kill me now? A hunger for something you can't identify?"

"No." Deep inside, all I had was a yearning to be with Noah.

"I don't think you ever will. And if you do, we'll work it out." He smiled as though he'd solved all our problems in one move. "Now, do you still want to leave?"

I don't know. I knew fear drove my decision to leave, but I felt like it was the only option, at least until I figured all this out. I couldn't see any other path. "Yes."

"Then it's settled. We leave." His smile widened as though he won some imaginary war between us, even though I was the one to invade his territory and threaten his people. "I just need to drop by the bar on our way out to give Liam the keys.

"Hang on. You're serious?"

He brushed his thumb along my bottom lip. "I love you, baby. For me, there's only ever been you. I can't imagine existing without you in my life. I'm coming with you."

My pulse quickened and tiny butterflies fluttered in my chest. "What about the bar? Your brothers? Your home is here."

He thought for a moment, and I almost held my breath waiting for his response. I wanted him to come with me, of course I did, but I'd never ask him to leave his family. No one should give up their family for the one they loved. Family was everything.

"My brothers understand. Liam's buying the bar from me." He swept a loose strand of hair behind my ear. "Some wise person once said home is where the heart is. Mia, my heart is yours, it has been for fifteen years, ever since I sensed you in the backyard of this house. Where you go, I go."

Could it be? The thought of leaving him made my chest ache, but the thought of staying freaked me out just as much. I was a hunter, his sworn enemy. But...what if by mating with him, we achieved what Joan couldn't? I so desperately wanted to be happy, to have him by my side as I figured all this out.

He bent, eye level with me. "Say yes, baby. Tell me you want this too."

I stared into those impossibly bright blue eyes, full of familiarity, comfort, and love. Was I still scared about becoming a hunter and what our future held? *Absolutely.* But I made a vow long ago that I'd take life into my own hands and make it my own. I wouldn't let my screwed-up childhood prevent me from becoming the woman I wanted to be. The woman I was meant to be.

And that woman wanted to be with Noah.

My heart fluttered as I smiled. "Yes." I placed my hands over his on my cheeks. "Yes. Okay. Let's do this."

He kissed me deep and hard, like he resealed the bond between us so it would never break. This kiss was more than a mating bond, this felt stronger, as though he not only vowed his protection and love for the rest of his life, but he also gave me his heart.

His full heart.

He eased back and smoothed his hands along my face to rest at the nape of my neck. His thumbs idly stroked my jaw. "Ash said he'll bring your car up one weekend if you want me to drive."

"I'd like that."

He kissed my forehead, lingering for a moment. "Let's get outta here."

With one hand, he grabbed my suitcase by the door and my hand with the other and led me to his truck. While he secured my belongings in the truck bed, I grabbed the two boxes of keepsakes from my car. The sight of Noah's packing boxes next to mine made my breath hitch.

He was really doing this. We were really doing this.

He paused glancing at me over the hood. "You ready?"

I forced a smile. "Yep."

Was I though?

His eyes narrowed, but he didn't say anything further. Instead, he hopped into the truck and I did the same. A few minutes down the road, we pulled into the parking lot of the bar.

"I just need to give Liam the keys." His lips rolled in. "And a stern talking to about not running my...*his*...bar into the ground."

Something heavy pressed against my chest, squeezing air from my lungs.

"I can give him your car keys too if you like?"

I nodded. "Sure." I fished them from my purse and handed them to Noah.

His fingers stilled around the keys clasped in my hand.

"Baby, are you okay?"

"Yeah. Sorry." I let him take the keys. "I'll send Ashton a text to thank him."

He nodded. "I'll be back in a second."

He jumped out the truck and jogged into the bar. Mid-morning, the bar and grill wasn't open for business yet, but I presumed Liam was there setting up as Noah had each day.

It all started at this bar. I first met Noah here. I came with such a clear plan and once I stepped into that bar, my world fell off its axis.

If I'd met Ashton somewhere else, would I have run into Noah? *Probably.* I suspected not only destiny, but Joan had a hand in ensuring Noah and I reconnected. A plan fifteen years in the making.

What if Noah's theory was true? What if by mating with him, we broke the hunter curse? I still had no urge to kill him or his brothers for their blood. Was this what Joan planned all along? Was this why she left me the house and not my mom?

I stared out the windshield to the road leading out of town.

What awaited me back in Seattle? *Nothing.* I'd lost my job. I'd almost burned through my savings by paying my share of the rent on my tiny apartment. I had no idea where my mother was, somewhere, with someone, most likely hunting shifters.

Nothing awaited me back in Seattle.

Everything that meant something to me was...right here in Woodland Falls. Everything Noah loved and cherished was here, too.

He told me wolves valued family above everything else. Yet, when it came down to it, he chose to leave his family for me. He chose to walk away from his life to be with his mate.

I clawed at my chest as the pressure increased so much I struggled to inhale.

I loved this man, more than I ever thought possible. I couldn't let him leave all this for me.

In the summer I spent here with Joan, I felt more connected with her than my own mother. With Joan's death, the Coles no longer had the concoction masking their scent. Without that protection, they were vulnerable to attack from other hunters. Ones that would kill them.

Joan wasn't just a hunter. She was the descendant of a powerful witch. We were so alike, not just in looks but I now suspected in values, and the belief to do what was right.

What if I...stayed? I had Joan's grimoire. I could use it to study, practice magic and develop my skill to protect the Coles and the entire shifter community. I could continue Joan's legacy and break the hunter curse for every family line of the original coven.

I'd no longer be a failure. I'd finally become a woman I was proud of.

A woman Joan would be proud of.

Reaching over to the ignition, I grabbed the keys to Noah's truck and got out. Inside the bar, I found Noah talking to Liam, pointing at various bottles with a clipboard in his hand. The scene threw me right back to the beginning, to that first night I came to Woodland Falls and saw him standing behind the bar.

I slid onto the same stool I sat on that night.

Noah glanced over his shoulder and smiled. "Sorry. I just need a few more minutes."

I dismissed his concern with a wave. "I'm staying right here."

He turned back to Liam, paused, then glanced at me. "What did you say?"

I placed my forearms on the bar top and settled in. "I think you should have a cocktail night every Friday. Maybe from seven? Start with a few classics to see if the locals like it before you go crazy ordering fancy glassware."

He moved closer to stand before me, a slight frown on his face. "Okay."

He didn't get it. I needed to be more obvious. "Maybe I could help, you know, we could test them before adding the cocktails to a menu. I could also help clear tables. You could teach me how to pour a beer."

"Mia, what are you saying?"

Deep breath.

For the first time in my life, I was about to put down roots. Not where I expected. In fact, somewhere totally unexpected. I didn't have a job, but given I still owned Joan's house, I could take my time finding work.

I glanced past Noah at his brother, who watched our exchange with a warm smile on his face. From the second I walked into this bar four weeks ago, the Cole family had been nothing but kind and welcoming.

Being here felt right. Staying here with Noah had never felt more right.

Liam's slight nod was the final reassurance I needed, to know I'd made the right decision.

I looked at Noah. "Let's stay."

His frown deepened. He tossed the clipboard on the counter. I swiveled my chair, tracking his every step as he rounded the bar to stand between my legs.

"I said I'd go with you. The bar is just a business." He brushed the back of his hand along my jaw. "You're what's important to me. You're my future."

My heart had never felt so full. He truly would give up everything for me.

"I know." I slid my hand down the tattoos on his arm until my fingers reached the lone wolf at his wrist. "Sitting in the parking lot I realized what's important to me."

"Cocktail night?"

I barked a laugh. "Yes. But what I want the most in my life, what I've been yearning for, is family. What you, your brothers and Ivy have, I want that. I'm nothing like my mother, and I won't turn out like her or those other psychos. I love you Noah Cole and I want a life with you. I want to be part of the Cole family."

"I love you too, baby." He kissed my forehead. "You're already part of the Cole family. It doesn't matter where we live. Don't stay here just for me."

I appreciated him saying that more than he'd ever

know. "I want to stay for us. I want to follow in my grand-mother's footsteps, embrace my witch heritage and protect shifters. I want to continue Joan's legacy together, right here in Woodland Falls."

He cupped my face in his. "Are you sure? 'Cause I would follow you anywhere."

"I know. But the only place I want you to follow me is back to the Whitcome House. Our house."

He held my gaze for precious heartbeats before taking my mouth with his. He kissed me like I was his salvation, the breath to his lungs. But little did he know, he was mine.

The kiss was full of love and commitment. Two souls finally reunited after so many years apart.

Still cradling my face between his hands, he drew back. "Are you definitely sure?"

I couldn't wipe the smile from my cheeks. "One-hundred percent."

Liam cleared his throat, leaning over the bar to dangle keys in the air between us. "Welcome back, you two." Liam raised his brows at me. "I'm glad you're stay-ing, 'cause the thought of making cocktails every Friday night freaked me the hell out."

Noah and I both laughed.

One laugh, one smile and my world righted itself again. Sure, we'd face challenges along the way, but together, I knew without a doubt that we'd make it through. Because nothing could ever rival the bonds of family and loyalty, and the power of love.

epilogue

Mia
Three months later.

Rolling my shoulders, I stretched my neck either side to get out the kinks. I'd locked myself in the shed of horrors for what felt like hours. The stiffness in my shoulders and back would agree. On the bright side, the evening darkness gave me the best excuse to practice my newly perfected fire-lighting witchy skills. Perfect for starting campfires, hearths, or a handful of candles to scatter around the shed. Tonight, I even levitated a few high in the roof space because...well, why not?

Look at me, becoming a cool freaking witch.

Witch. Not hunter.

If only I could master the concoction my grand-mother made for the Cole family to mask their shifter scent. I sighed a heavy breath. I'd been at it for days. After following Joan's instructions didn't work, I tried adding the ingredients in a different order, tinkering with the quantities, summoning a demon.

Just kidding. I didn't do that last part. Demons don't exist, right?

Regardless, no matter what I tried, the concoction never magically morphed into the dark crimson color Joan described in her grimoire. No point having fancy witchy fire-starting skills if hunters killed everyone I love.

Already, it'd been too long since the Cole family digested their last dose. What if another hunter came to town? What if they found them?

What if my mother...

Nope. Not going there. Summoning a demon was a walk in the woods compared to dealing with that woman.

Summer had come and gone, and I half expected my mother to contest Joan's will and make a claim for the estate. But she hadn't. Just as well. If she ever showed her face in Woodland Falls, I doubt the Coles would welcome her with open arms.

Honestly, I wouldn't either.

I trailed my index finger over the ink scribbled in Joan's grimoire. The thick parchment had faded to sepia over time, the pages crinkled at the edges. Joan had made so many annotations over the page, I presumed, as she perfected the spell—different herbs, bases, methods, and her thoughts on incubation.

Eventually, she'd gotten it right. The finished enchantment was on the page right in front of me. Why was it so hard to make?

Time wasn't on my side. Especially with Ivy and Liam's baby due any day now.

I needed to protect them. My family.

My finger paused on the word 'blood'. Noah had mentioned they continued to supply Joan with blood long after their father had died. Not to support Joan's hunter addiction or her thirst for immortality, but for the concoction she made to protect them.

I peered over my shoulder at the two remaining vials of blood in the open cabinet. Was the blood too old? Contaminated? Was it even shifter blood?

Would I know the difference?

Tiny prickles danced along my nape a second before I sensed Noah approach the doorway. I paused a moment before turning, preparing my heart for the burst that happened each time I caught sight of him. It always did. I couldn't help it. I mean, that rugged jean and T-shirt combo made a woman weak at the knees. Throw in his sleeve of wolf tattoos and our mate bond? This girl had no hope.

I pivoted when the barrier spanning the doorway pulsed with deep orange, before vanishing as Noah crossed the threshold.

Without saying a word, he strode right up to me, cupped my jaw in his powerful hands and took my mouth with his. Intense, all-consuming need flowed through our mate bond, as though he hadn't touched me for years. We'd been apart a few hours while he worked his shift at the bar, but hey, I didn't complain. I savored every moment I had with him.

His tongue glided over mine, reigniting the soul-deep fire inside me. Pinpricks of light danced before my eyes as my knees buckled, sinking into his embrace. I surrendered to every sensation sparking and combusting between us.

Too soon, Noah slowed down and eased back to rest his forehead against mine. "I needed that."

I swooned like a teenager, not a badass witch in training. So embarrassing. "So, you think just because you live here now, you can waltz in and kiss me whenever you want?"

I bit the inside of my lip, holding back a grin.

Noah drew back enough to brace his hands on the bench beside me, caging me in. Those intense eyes burned right to the center of my soul. "Yeah, that's exactly what I thought."

I willed my heart rate to steady, so I didn't climb the man like a tree. "Well...I guess that's okay."

His lips hitched up at the corner. "I'm glad you agree. Because I plan to do it every opportunity I get."

"Suits me just fine."

Lowering his head, he skimmed his lips over mine with the briefest kiss that left me aching for more. That man knew exactly how to turn me into a gooey mess.

And I loved it.

Attempting to regain some composure, I re-diverted our conversation. "How was cocktail night?"

Noah stepped back to lean his butt against the bench behind him. "It's official. Liam can't make cocktails for shit. I dunno what he does, but he's now on beer and bourbon duty only."

I laughed. Friday night cocktails were a hit in Woodland Falls. Usually, I perched on a barstool next to Ivy and chatted the night away while we tested Noah's new alcoholic and non-alcoholic creations.

But not tonight. Tonight, I mixed concoctions of a different kind.

Noah tipped his chin to the mortar and pestle on the bench beside me. "How's it going?"

He'd never pressured me to hurry, which I appreciated more than he knew, but I sensed his unease. Each day without the concoction put his, *our,* family at risk.

"How often did Ash give Joan blood?"

He tilted his head, thinking for a moment. "A few times a year, I think. A day or so after, she'd give us a new vial."

Exactly what I thought. The blood stored in the cupboard was too old. I needed a fresh batch.

A knot twisted in my gut. Would fresh blood ignite the sick hunter part of me? If exposed to it, would I crave the kill? Would I want to murder my mate?

Noah believed we'd broken the hunter's curse on the Whitcome side by sealing our mate bond. But what if we hadn't? What if we only *thought* we had? What if I didn't experience the hunter urges because I'd never exposed myself to shifter blood?

Sure, when I tried to heal Ash after the hunter attacked, I didn't rip apart his vein like a crazed vampire. But that happened before Noah healed me using his blood. Before he activated the hunter curse.

Noah gravitated back into my personal space and curled a finger under my chin, lifting my gaze to his. "Baby, what's wrong?"

"I..." I swallowed.

That knot in my belly gravitated upward to lodge in the base of my throat.

I couldn't do it. The risk was too high. What if something went wrong? What if I...

Noah's brows drew together as concern and his primal need to protect me trickled through our bond. He didn't even know what was wrong, yet I sensed him ready to tear apart the invisible threat just to make sure I was safe.

He'd do anything to protect me.

For a moment, I lost myself in his bright blue eyes. My mate. The man I'd fallen so in love with, I couldn't imagine my life without him. Without all the Cole family. In a few short months, they'd welcomed me with open arms and had become *my* family.

I needed to trust that Noah was right. We had broken the hunter curse. Because, when it came down to it, I'd do anything to protect him. All of them.

I was a badass Whitcome witch. If I could survive a childhood with my mother, fight off a hunter, and almost die trying to save a wolf shifter, I could do this damn spell.

Strength soared through my veins, filling me with determination. "I think the spell isn't working because I need...fresh Cole blood."

"Okay." He drew out the word. "Are you up for that? That's one helluva test."

The lump thickened in my throat, but I swallowed it down.

"I've followed Joan's instructions and so far, it hasn't worked. I have to at least try." My heart thumped. "Unless...you think it's too risky?"

His gaze softened as he brushed his knuckles along my jaw. "I trust you."

That didn't answer my question, but I let it slide.

Before I talked myself out of it, I added a new batch of ingredients in the mortar and pestle. Herbs, the weird purple powder, drops of the orange solution, and a dried flower from a black elderberry. Using the pestle, I muddled them together until it resembled a thick paste.

Next, came the blood.

My gaze drifted to the ancient dagger I originally found next to Joan's grimoire. Every time I curled my fingers around the hilt, raw power flooded my veins, coursing through my body, igniting my witch heritage. A side I'd become more comfortable with over the past few months.

With the dagger in one hand, I held out the other for Noah's hand. He didn't hesitate. His trust level was off the charts.

Holding his wrist over the mortar, I pressed the tip of the dagger against his skin. My hand shook so much, I struggled to hold it steady.

This was a bad idea.

I couldn't do it.

Just as I considered withdrawing the blade, Noah placed his free hand over mine. He guided the dagger along his wrist, slicing a thin, straight line. Blood pooled at the cut before sliding into the waiting mortar.

My gaze zeroed in on the drops, while I mentally assessed every slight change inside me. Mainly, searching for any sudden urges to drink Noah's bright red life-force.

Nothing.

Well, that wasn't quite true. Hot fluttering sensations bloomed low in my belly while each nerve ending sparked and crackled. My breath quickened. I dragged my gaze up to Noah's. His eyes darkened to a deep blue, filled with not just heat and desire, but something resembling raw need. I'd witnessed this look enough times now to know it always resulted in him doing wicked things that left me in a state of pleasured bliss.

Tempting. So, so tempting.

But now wasn't the time for nakedness, no matter how much I craved it.

As the cut healed, I placed the dagger on the bench and let go of his wrist. I grabbed the pestle and combined his shifter blood with the other ingredients. Power hummed from my hands into the mortar, just as it had every other attempt. But this time the magic built to a crescendo. Surface bubbles popped, splattering me—

Crimson light burst from the mortar.

I jolted backwards, bumping into Noah. One second light illuminated the shed, the next it vanished. Inching forward, I leaned over the bench to peek into the mortar.

The bubbles eased to a simmer in the liquid.

Liquid. Dark red liquid.

"That's it," I squealed. "I did it."

Noah moved closer behind me, pressing his front

against my back, hovering his mouth at my ear. "I never doubted you. Not for a second."

He pressed a soft kiss below my ear, reawakening the tingles between my legs.

"Do you have an urge to kill me?"

I angled my head to one side, giving his lips more access. Warm kisses trailed down my exposed shoulder.

Internally, I rescanned my feelings and emotions. Triumph, hope, relief. Freaking desire. But no blood thirst.

We'd truly broken the hunter's curse.

Before he distracted me with his mouth again, I cradled the mortar in both hands and twisted in Noah's embrace to face him. "I've never been more relieved to not want to kill you. But you might kill me for how disgusting it tastes."

He barked a laugh. Without hesitation, he tipped the mortar to his mouth and drank a mouthful. I waited. Mainly to make sure I hadn't screwed up and turned him into a demon. Or summoned one for real.

Noah slid the mortar onto the bench beside me. "Tastes as awful as Joan's version did."

A soft smile warmed my cheeks. I'd done it. I'd recreated the spell that would protect them from hunters.

Noah slipped his hand in mine, giving it a light squeeze. "Joan would be so proud of you. *I'm* proud of you."

An invisible fist clenched my heart.

"This changes everything. Think of how many shifters we can protect. Not just your brothers and Ivy, but other packs. We can help other original families break the hunter's curse. We can end the hunters for good."

He brushed his fingers along my jaw. "One day at a time."

"You're right." Turning back to the bench, I distributed the concoction into three waiting vials before popping on a cork seal. "We need to get these to your brothers and Ivy."

From behind, Noah's arms snaked around my middle, holding me firm against him. "First, I want to give you something."

I smirked. Was that code for sex? If so, I might consider it. "Oh, really?"

Something made me glance down at his hand. My breath stalled. Nestled inside his palm was a beautiful diamond ring.

"Noah," I whispered, turning to face him.

His eyes beamed with pride. My mind flew back to the first time he took me to the waterfall where he gave me the same look. As though I were a beautiful and magical creation. But back then, I hadn't realized that look was love. I also hadn't realized that I felt it too.

"Every day, I'm so honored and fucking humbled that you're my mate. I spent fifteen years waiting for you, and I want to spend the rest of our lives showing you how worthy I am of your love." He held the ring between us. "And that starts by making you my wife."

I loved this man more than anything in this world. He brought my heart back to life, made me feel safe and protected, and showed me what it was like to be part of a true family. And I never wanted to let him go.

Marriage was never something I'd considered in my future, but now, with Noah, I couldn't imagine existing without it. Everything felt as though it had finally fallen into place.

"I love you, Noah Cole. Yes, I'll become your wife."

He slipped the ring on my finger before gripping my hips and lifting me onto the edge of the workbench. "Now, kiss me."

The End!

Craving more small-town shifters?
Grab Reclaim and get ready to swoon over these Cedar Valley Bear shifters.

Craving more sexy shifters? Grab Reclaim today.

Can't wait for the next book? Fall for Cassie's award-winning steamy bad boy angel series, The Fallen Guardians! Where the heroes bring down Hell for the women they love.

Start the series today.

ACKNOWLEDGMENTS

Firstly, a huge congratulations to Nancy C for choosing the winning town name of Woodland Falls – it's perfect! I hope you love Noah and Mia's story!

A big thank you to the members of my Facebook Reader Group (Cassie's Log Cabin) – you're awesome! Thank you for cheering me on, talking about my books and pestering me for more. Your support means the world to me.

Also, thank you to every reader who reads, reviews and/or promotes my books! Salvation is the beginning of a new and exciting adventure, and I can't wait to share more of the Small Town Packs series with you.

Cassie x

ALSO BY CASSIE LAELYN

The Fallen Guardians

Unforsaken (Book 1)

Unforgotten (Book 2)

Unseen (Book 3)

Untamed (Book 4) coming 2021!

Small Town Packs

Salvation

Reclaim

Awaken (coming soon!)

ABOUT THE AUTHOR

Cassie is an award-winning paranormal romance author living in sunny Queensland, Australia with her husband and two BMX-crazy boys.

She has a passion for crafting stories involving loyal, otherwordly characters in need of love and redemption. She's also a self-confessed chocoholic and a huge sucker for an angsty, gut-wrenching happily ever after.

When she isn't narrating imaginary characters, Cassie loves binging on TV shows, spending time at the beach, and curling up listening to the rain.

Join Cassie's newsletter (www.cassielaelyn.com) to stay up to date with release information, including the next instalment in her award-winning, steamy paranormal romance series, The Fallen Guardians.

You can also stalk @cassielaelyn

Facebook ~ Instagram ~ Twitter
BookBub ~ Goodreads